"What's all this?" the chef asked. . . .

"This young fellow," the cop said, "was a witness at a crime. I just came to tell him we arrested the punks who did it."

LeRoy waited until the chef had walked away. Then he turned to the cop. "Man, I told you, I'm not going to say anything!"

"You might as well, LeRoy," the cop said. "B. J. already thinks you pointed him out."

"He's going to cut me, that's what he's going to do!" LeRoy said.

"He can't cut you if he's in jail, LeRoy. Think about that."

"Well, you just keep him in jail, then."

"The judge set his bail at $10,000, LeRoy," the cop said. "He can't make it. So he's in jail to stay."

"I'm glad to hear that."

"The judge set Elton's bail at $2,500. His brother came up with the money. Elton's out on bail."

"He is?"

"And so is Pettaway," the cop said.

"Where does that leave me?" LeRoy asked.

The cop met his eyes. . . . "I'm sorry, LeRoy."

"Well-told story with believable characters. . . ."
—*School Library Journal*

"A strong and sympathetic character . . . the plot is nicely knit. . . ."
—*Bulletin of the Center for Children's Books*

LeRoy
and the Old Man

by

W.E. Butterworth

Vagabond Books

SCHOLASTIC BOOK SERVICES
New York Toronto London Auckland Sydney Tokyo

ISBN: 0-590-32635-X

12 11 10 9 8 7 6 5 4 3 2 1   6   2 3 4 5 6 7/8

For Miriam Lee,
Who has given the joy of reading to
a lot of people who would otherwise
have gone through life without it.

CHAPTER
1

The cops were waiting for him when he got home from work. One of them was a uniformed Chicago policeman, assigned to the housing project. The other was a white man everybody called "the junkie." He went around in dirty and torn clothes and without a shave, trying to look like a junkie. He didn't fool anybody. Everyone knew he was a plainclothes cop.

They were waiting for him in the corridor. The uniformed cop was standing by the door to the fire stairs, holding his nightstick in his hands, and the junkie was leaning against the wall.

LeRoy knew they were waiting for him the moment he passed the junkie. The junkie pushed himself off the wall and started after LeRoy. The uniformed cop stepped into the middle of the corridor.

"Got a minute, LeRoy?" the junkie asked, grabbing LeRoy's arm and pushing him through the door to the stairs. "We'd like to talk to you."

"I didn't do anything," LeRoy said.

"Nobody said you did," the junkie replied.

"But you did hear about the old lady getting ripped off on the sixth floor?" the uniformed cop asked.

"No," LeRoy said. "I didn't." It was a lie. He'd seen what had happened to her.

All of a sudden, LeRoy found himself bouncing off the concrete blocks of the wall. The uniformed cop had done it, pushed him so quickly LeRoy hadn't even seen it coming. Now the cop had one end of his nightstick pushing against LeRoy's throat.

"It's not nice to tell lies, LeRoy," he said. "Didn't your mother ever tell you that?"

"Hey, brother!"

"Don't you call me brother, punk," the uniformed cop said. "You're no brother of mine."

"The thing is, LeRoy," the junkie said, "that Mrs. Carson — that's the lady who got ripped off, in case you didn't know her name — well, Mrs. Carson identified you. I just came from the hospital."

"I don't know what you're talking about," LeRoy said.

The uniformed cop pushed a little harder with the end of his nightstick.

"LeRoy, don't interrupt," he said. "It's not polite to interrupt."

"Mrs. Carson said we should look for a young guy, skinny, maybe six-foot-four, and neatly dressed," the junkie said. "That sound like you, LeRoy?"

"I never touched that old lady!" LeRoy said.

"Who said you touched her?" the junkie asked. "I didn't say you touched her, LeRoy. All I said was that Mrs. Carson said we should find a guy who looks like you."

"I don't know anything about it," LeRoy said.

"Don't lie to us, LeRoy," said the uniformed cop. "When punks like you lie to me, I get mad and lose my temper."

"Where were you at half-past ten last night, LeRoy?" the junkie asked him.

"Home," LeRoy said.

"Home? You mean here in the development?"

"Yeah."

"You didn't go out?"

"I went to the movies."

"You went to the movies?"

"That's what I said."

"What time?"

"I don't know. Maybe eight o'clock."

"And then you came right home?"

"Yeah, I came right home."

"Which means that you got here a little after ten, right?" the junkie asked.

"I suppose," LeRoy said.

"And when you got off the elevator on the sixth floor, you saw those bums ripping off Mrs. Carson, right?"

LeRoy didn't answer.

"Friends of yours, are they?" the junkie said.

"I don't know what you're talking about," LeRoy said.

"They cut Mrs. Carson, LeRoy," the uniformed cop said. "Stealing her purse and her watch wasn't

3

enough. They had to show what tough guys they were by cutting that nice old lady.

"That means when we collar them, LeRoy, they're going to be charged with assault with a deadly weapon. It's not just simple purse snatching."

"What's that got to do with me?"

"We can do this easy, LeRoy, or we can do it hard. It'll be easy if you just tell us who they were."

"What makes you think I know?"

"Mrs. Carson says you saw it, LeRoy," said the junkie. "She says that just after they knocked her down, she saw you getting off the elevator."

"I didn't see anything," LeRoy said.

"And you didn't call the cops and tell them there was a mugging?" the uniformed cop asked.

"No," LeRoy said.

"You're not a very good liar, LeRoy," the junkie said. "Don't you know that when you call the police emergency number, they make a recording of it? That was your voice, all right."

"All right," LeRoy said. "So I called the cops."

"And you saw who cut that old lady?"

"Yeah, I saw them."

"Who were they, LeRoy?"

"I don't know," LeRoy said. That was another lie. And it must have shown on his face, for the uniformed cop jabbed him with the nightstick again.

"Quit lying to me, LeRoy," he said.

LeRoy, angry now, said what was on his mind. "Look, you think I'm crazy? If I tell you who did that, they'll really get me. You know who did it; you go arrest them. You just leave me out of it."

The junkie and the uniformed cop looked at each

4

other. The junkie threw up his hands in disgust. The uniformed cop took the nightstick out of LeRoy's throat. Then he suddenly grabbed LeRoy's jacket and pulled his face close.

"You make me sick, boy," he said. "I call you 'boy' because you sure ain't no man." Then he pushed him away, a hard shove. "Get out of my sight."

LeRoy walked past the junkie, who looked at him with cold eyes, and went back into the corridor and over to the elevator. He felt a little sick to his stomach. He had always sort of liked the uniformed cop. He was tall and skinny like LeRoy. They had Watusi blood in them. LeRoy had read in school that some people believed the Watusi were descendants of the ancient Egyptians, the people who had built the pyramids. That was interesting to think about, even if he wasn't sure it was true.

He pushed the button for the sixth floor and the door slid closed. It smelled bad in the elevator, and somebody had scratched "Wolves" in the paint with a screwdriver or a knife. "Wolves" was the name of the gang in this part of the housing development. He knew who they were. The guys who had assaulted Mrs. Carson were Wolves.

The elevator jerked to a stop and the door slid open. LeRoy stepped into the corridor and started toward his apartment. All of a sudden, the door to the fire stairs opened and three guys came out. They were Mrs. Carson's attackers: Elton, Howard, and B.J. LeRoy knew them well enough. They had been in elementary school together. They were all wearing blue denim jackets with the face of a wolf stitched

5

on the back. The word *Wolves* was spelled out with little metal studs above the wolf's face, and they had their names written the same way on the front of the jackets.

"Well, if it isn't good old LeRoy," B.J. said. "How's the weather up there, LeRoy?"

"How goes it, B.J.?" LeRoy said, and kept walking. B.J. put his hand on LeRoy's sleeve and stopped him.

"What's the hurry, man? You don't have time for your old friends?"

"I got off work late," LeRoy said. "I got stuff to do."

"You got a job, LeRoy? What kind of a job?"

"Same old job," LeRoy replied. "I work down at the Del Monte Cafeteria."

"Doing what, LeRoy?" B.J. asked. But before LeRoy could answer, the door to the stairs opened again and another Wolf, a younger one, Howard's cousin Stanley, came into the corridor. He was out of breath. LeRoy knew he had just run up the stairs. He had probably been sitting in the stairwell near the ground floor while LeRoy had been talking to the cops.

"Well?" B.J. asked.

"He didn't tell them nothing," Stanley said. B.J. nodded, and turned to face LeRoy.

"We saw the cops," B.J. said. "They was up here before, knocking on your door. Your mother told them you wasn't home from work yet. So we figured they just might wait for you downstairs."

LeRoy didn't say anything.

"What did they want to talk to you about, LeRoy?" B.J. asked.

6

"They wanted to know if I knew who ripped off some old woman," LeRoy said.

"But you didn't have anything to tell them, huh?" B.J. asked.

"I told them I didn't know what they were talking about," LeRoy said.

"No, he didn't, either," Stanley said.

"What, exactly, did he tell them?" B.J. asked. He motioned with his head, and Elton and Howard grabbed LeRoy.

"Hey, man, let me go!" LeRoy said, but he didn't struggle. B.J. took a knife — a switchblade with a long, thin blade — out of his sock and flicked it open.

"He told them he knew who done it," Stanley said.

"LeRoy said that?" B.J. said. "That wasn't too smart of you, LeRoy." He stepped over to LeRoy, grabbed one of the buttons on his leather coat, and sliced it off with the knife.

"I told them I wasn't going to say anything," LeRoy said.

"Did he say that, too, Stanley?" B.J. asked.

"Yeah, he told the cops that if he said anything, he knew he was going to get cut."

"Well, that was smart. I'm not surprised. After all, LeRoy did stay in school and graduate, didn't you, LeRoy?"

"Look, B.J.," LeRoy said. "I didn't tell the cops anything, and I won't tell the cops anything."

"You told them you saw something, though, didn't you, LeRoy?" B.J. said. He pulled another button away from LeRoy's coat and sliced that one off, too. "You shouldn't have told them even that much."

B.J. turned to Stanley. "What did the cops say?" he asked.

"The tall, skinny one said LeRoy made him sick," Stanley said. "And he called him 'boy.' Said he was calling him 'boy' because he wasn't no man."

"And what did the junkie say?" B.J. asked.

"Nothing," Stanley said.

"And that's what you should say, LeRoy," B.J. said. "Nothing. In case the cops should talk to you again. You understand that, LeRoy?"

"I'm not going to say anything," LeRoy said.

"I *know* you're not," B.J. said. "Because you're smart, LeRoy. You went and finished school. What I'm saying, LeRoy, is that you're smart enough to know that if you did say something, you'd likely get cut yourself. You know what I mean, LeRoy, when I say *cut*?" Then he grabbed LeRoy's jacket again. This time he didn't slice off a button. He jabbed the point of his knife into the leather and ripped upward. He cut a slash five inches long in the jacket.

If the other three weren't there, LeRoy thought angrily, I'd make him eat that blade. But the other three Wolves were there, and if he started something, he'd wind up getting hurt.

"That's what I mean when I say *cut*, LeRoy," B.J. said.

The Wolves laughed. LeRoy realized he was shaking with anger.

"See you around, LeRoy," B.J. said. He closed the switchblade by pressing it against his leg, then turned away and stepped into the elevator. The other Wolves followed him.

LeRoy continued down the corridor, took the key from his pocket, and opened the door to his apartment.

His mother was sitting at the kitchen table, drinking a cup of coffee. When she saw him come through the door, she got up quickly and walked over to him. She was still wearing the white uniform she wore at work in the bakery.

"The cops were here looking for you," she said. "What for?"

"Nothing," LeRoy said.

"What do you mean, nothing?" his mother asked.

"They thought I saw something, is all," LeRoy said.

"Saw what?"

"Some guys ripped off Mrs. Carson," LeRoy said. "That old lady who lives in 606."

"I know Mrs. Carson," his mother said. "Did you see it happen, LeRoy?"

"No," LeRoy replied. He didn't like lying to his mother, but he didn't want to frighten her.

"You're sure? Then you better call the station house and tell them."

"I already told them," LeRoy said. "They were waiting for me downstairs when I came in."

When LeRoy saw the relief on his mother's face, he didn't feel quite so bad about lying to her. Then she saw the rip in his jacket.

"What happened to your jacket?" she asked. "Oh, LeRoy, it's practically brand-new and you paid so much money for it!"

"I fell down," he said.

"It's ruined," his mother said. "Oh, LeRoy!"

What he wanted to say was, "Better the jacket than my skin." But, of course, he couldn't.

CHAPTER
2

LeRoy was a salad man at the Del Monte
Cafeteria. He'd started out washing dishes.
Then they'd made him a busboy, and after
he'd done that for a while, the boss had told
him he could go one of two ways. He could start
out as a waiter on the night shift and maybe work
his way up to "front room assistant manager." Or
he could go back in the kitchen and learn to be a
cook, beginning as a salad man.

LeRoy hadn't thought there was much future, or
much fun, in either carrying people's trays to their
tables or working the cash register in the front room.
And he liked food. So they started him off in the
kitchen, at the salad counter.

In one way, it was sort of a stupid job. There
was a Del Monte Cafeteria menu book that told you
exactly how to make each one of the ten different

salads they put out every day on the counters. All you had to do was follow the directions.

On the other hand, the more you did it, the better you got at it. One of the assistant chefs had taught LeRoy how to sharpen and use a French knife. He'd been a little awkward at first, but now he could go through a head of lettuce with that big knife just as fast and fancy as the guy who taught cooking on television. And while he was working, particularly during lunch and dinner — when he had to keep an eye on the line to see which salads the customers had taken, and then make more of them so there would always be a full selection on display — the time passed very quickly.

He worked at a little wooden counter just inside the kitchen, dressed in cook's whites and a big starched hat. After he'd been on the job a couple of days, he'd brought his transistor radio to work and put it on the shelf over the counter. The assistant chef told him he couldn't play it, but the chef said that he could. "Providing you don't play it loud, slim," he said. "And none of that thump, bang, crash, hard-rock music."

Any music, even country and western played soft, was better than no music at all. So the radio stayed. And over the radio, on the twelve o'clock news the next day, while he was pushing tomatoes through the slicing machine, he got the bad news:

"Police today arrested three young men, residents of the Hoover Housing Project, and charged them with armed robbery and assault with a deadly weapon. They were charged in the case of Mrs. Sarah-Mae Carson, aged sixty-five, who was mugged and stabbed in the housing project two days ago. All of those arrested, B.J. Norton, eighteen, Elton Davidson, nineteen, and Howard Pettaway, eighteen, are allegedly members of a gang called the Wolves."

The first thing LeRoy felt was relief. He was glad the cops had grabbed them. And he was glad they had done it without his help — that he was out of it.

But that good feeling deserted LeRoy as quickly as it had come. He knew B.J. wouldn't believe he hadn't told the cops anything. B.J. would think he had identified them. And B.J. was just crazy and mean enough to carry out his threat.

At half-past three, while he was trying not to think about B.J.'s revenge, while he was cutting slashes in radishes so that when they were put in cold salted water, the cut pieces would curl up and look good at the dinner salads, the skinny cop from the housing project showed up at the Del Monte Cafeteria. The assistant chef brought him over to LeRoy. Then he ran and told the chef, who came right away.

"What's all this?" the chef asked, and LeRoy didn't like the look on his face.

"This young fellow," the cop said, "was a witness at a crime. I just came to tell him we arrested the punks who did it."

"He wasn't involved, then?" the chef asked. It wasn't hard to guess what the chef had been thinking.

"No, not at all," the cop said. "He was just a witness. He happened to walk up when these punks were jumping an old lady."

"Then what do you want with him?" the chef asked.

"I just wanted to tell him we made the arrest. And that the district attorney's office will be coming to see him, to get his statement."

"Well, okay, then," the chef said. "I'm glad that's all it is. I won't have anybody working for me who's having trouble with the cops."

"LeRoy's not having any trouble with us," the cop said. "He's what you would call a respectable citizen doing his duty by testifying against these animals."

"Well, make it quick, will you?" the chef said. "We've got things to do before they start coming in for supper."

LeRoy waited until the chef had walked away. Then he turned to the cop. "Man, I told you, I'm not going to say anything!"

"You might as well, LeRoy," the cop said. "B.J. already thinks you pointed him out."

"He's going to cut me, that's what he's going to do!" LeRoy said.

"He can't cut you if he's in jail, LeRoy. Think about that."

"Well, you just keep him in jail, then."

"The judge set his bail at $10,000, LeRoy," the cop said. "He can't make it. So he's in jail to stay."

"I'm glad to hear that."

"The judge set Elton's bail at $2,500. His brother came up with the money. Elton's out on bail."

"He is?"

"And so is Pettaway," the cop said.

"Where does that leave me?" LeRoy asked.

"I had a little chat with Elton and Howard while they were getting their stuff back at the jail," the cop said. "I told them if they went near you, LeRoy, I'd personally make them eat my nightstick."

14

"You think you scared them?" LeRoy asked.

The cop met his eyes. "About as much as I scared you when we had our talk," he said. "I'm sorry, LeRoy."

"Those guys, all the Wolves, are going to get me," LeRoy said.

"Maybe not," said the cop. "Just be careful. Keep an eye open. Don't get caught in a dark alley."

"Thanks a lot," LeRoy said. "There's twenty, thirty, maybe even more of them."

"I know," the cop said. "That's really why I came over to see you. And I wanted you to know that we tried, Moriarity and me, to keep B.J. from thinking you pointed him out."

"Who's Moriarity?" LeRoy asked.

"The white guy you call the junkie," the cop said. "The detective who was with me."

"B.J. thinks I told you," LeRoy said.

"I'm afraid so," the cop said. "Be careful, LeRoy."

After work, the closer the bus brought him to the housing project, the more afraid LeRoy became. He was sure the Wolves would be waiting for him. Once off the bus, he had to force himself not to run through the walkways to his building.

When he got to his building, he relaxed a little. There was a police car parked outside. He didn't think Elton or Howard would try anything with cops around.

As usual, he took the elevator to the sixth floor and walked down the corridor toward his apartment. Approaching the apartment, he noticed that the door was open. When he got closer, he saw why. The door had been broken open. Somebody — obviously the

Wolves — had smashed it in with one of the heavy fire extinguishers that hung on the wall.

When he walked through the door, he found the junkie and two uniformed cops, the ones, he guessed from the police car downstairs. The upholstery on the couch and the armchair had been cut. The stuffing, a gray-white mess, was sticking out.

"Where's my mother?" LeRoy asked.

"In there," the junkie said. "Packing."

His mother heard his voice. She came running out, crying, and wrapped her arms around him.

"LeRoy," she cried, "why didn't you tell me?"

"I didn't want to worry you," he said gently. Then, over her shoulder, he asked the junkie, "What are you going to do about it?"

"What can we do?" the junkie replied. "There were no witnesses."

"They beat in a steel door with a fire extinguisher and nobody heard them?" LeRoy replied.

"That's what they say, LeRoy," the junkie said. "We asked everybody on this floor."

"We're getting out of here," his mother said. "We're going to a hotel. I got some clothes packed for you."

"How are we going to afford a hotel?" LeRoy asked.

"Just for the night," his mother said. "Maybe a day or two. Then we'll find some other place to live."

"I think that's a good idea, LeRoy," the junkie said. "I told your mother what this is all about. I think you should get out of here, at least for a while."

LeRoy didn't want to say it in front of his mother, but he wondered what good moving out was going to do. The Wolves knew where he worked. They'd get at him there.

The junkie drove them to a small hotel on the North Side in his unmarked car. He even followed them to their room, carrying one of the suitcases. He gave LeRoy's mother a card.

"You can call this number any time of the day or night," he said. "And you're just around the corner from the station house here. I don't think you'll have any more trouble."

LeRoy's mother thanked the junkie and watched him leave. Then she sat down on the bed and folded her arms over her stomach.

"We'll find another place to live," LeRoy said. "Maybe even a nicer place."

"You're getting out of here, that's what you're going to do," his mother said.

"What do you mean?" LeRoy asked. "Where am I going to go?"

"You're going to your father's father," his mother said.

"Don't be silly," LeRoy said. "He don't even know who I am."

LeRoy's father had disappeared when LeRoy had been in the sixth grade. He just hadn't come home from work one night. When his mother had called the place where he worked, they told her that they had let him go. And that was the last they ever saw or heard of him.

"He's your grandfather," his mother said. "And Pass Christian, Mississippi, is a long way from here."

"I'm not going to Mississippi," LeRoy said.

"Yes, you are," his mother said firmly. "And you're going on the next bus."

17

"And what happens to you?"

"Nothing happens to me," his mother replied. "I keep right on working. I get us another place to live. And when the trial is over, you can come back. If you don't show up to testify, maybe they'll leave you alone."

"I'm not going anywhere," LeRoy said.

"You want to stay here and get hurt? Maybe killed?" his mother said. "You don't have any choice, LeRoy. I don't want you dead or cut up."

"What about my job?" LeRoy protested.

"What good is a job, if you're in no condition to work?" his mother asked. "You're going to your grandfather's, and you're going right now." She got up from the bed and went to her purse. "Have you got any money?" she asked.

"I got my check tonight," LeRoy said.

"I got enough for the bus ticket and for you to buy food on the way," his mother said. "And a little more. You just sign over your paycheck to me. I'll get it cashed later."

"Momma," LeRoy said, "I don't want to go."

"For God's sake, LeRoy, can't you see it's the only way we've got out of this mess?" she said. "And it won't be for long. Only until the trial's over. Then you can come back."

"What I should do," LeRoy said angrily, "is get me a knife and do some cutting of my own."

His mother slapped him on the face.

"Don't you ever say something like that again," she said. He looked down at her and saw the tears in her eyes. Then she hugged him, and he held her until he felt that she had stopped crying.

Two hours later, he was on a Trailways bus headed south. The trip to New Orleans took twenty-eight hours. He was too tall for the seat, and every once in a while he had to get up and stretch his legs. Every couple of hours, the bus made a rest stop and he got something to eat. At one rest stop, at a bus terminal, he got a schedule and saw that he would arrive in New Orleans at two o'clock in the morning. The bus from New Orleans to Pass Christian left New Orleans at 7:15. He'd have to sit around a bus terminal for five hours in the dead of night.

When the bus got to New Orleans, LeRoy took his time getting off. With five hours to wait, there was no reason to hurry. His bag had been checked through to Pass Christian, so he didn't have to worry about that. He got off the bus and decided to have a look around.

It was a strange kind of bus station. Trains used it, too. He walked outside. There wasn't much going on. There were a lot of tall buildings, hotels and office buildings, new ones, he thought. It didn't look much different from home. He could probably get along all right here. But Pass Christian, Mississippi? He could guess what that was going to be like.

LeRoy went back into the combined bus-train station, found the restroom, and washed up. Then he went into the waiting room again, wondering if he could catch a few minutes' sleep on one of the chairs.

A funny-looking old guy came up to him. He was wearing an old-fashioned gabardine suit, a snap-on bow tie, and an old-fashioned hat with the brim turned up all around. He was nearly as wide as he was tall. He looked as if he were about to burst the seams of the suit, but it was muscle, LeRoy saw, not fat.

"What's your name, boy?" the old guy said.

"What's it to you?" LeRoy replied.

"Well, if it's LeRoy Chambers, I'm your grandfather," he said.

CHAPTER
3

"You're my grandfather?" LeRoy asked.

"If you're LeRoy Chambers, I am," the old man replied.

"I'm LeRoy Chambers," LeRoy said.

The old man put out his hand. LeRoy shook it. It was as tough and rough as the sole of a boot.

"I figured I'd meet you here," the old man said. "Otherwise you'd have to wait around until seven in the morning."

"Yeah," LeRoy said.

"Your mother called last night," the old man said. "Told me you were coming."

"She tried to call you before the bus left," LeRoy said. "There was no answer."

"I didn't get in until late," the old man said. "The engine acted up."

His grandfather wasn't what LeRoy expected. He had expected him to look like his father. What he

21

remembered of his father was that he was tall and skinny. His grandfather was short and stocky.

"Is it all right that I came?" LeRoy asked.

"It is if you're not running from the police," his grandfather said. "You mother didn't make a whole lot of sense on the telephone. She was all excited and crying."

"I'm not running from the police," LeRoy said. But as he said it, he wondered if he was telling the truth. His mother, he remembered, hadn't told the junkie what she was thinking, about sending him out of town.

"Didn't you bring a bag?" LeRoy's grandfather asked.

"I checked it through to Pass Christian," LeRoy said. He pronounced it as in "Christian church."

"We say that 'Chris-tea-ann,'" the old man said. "Pass Chris-tea-ann. It's French." He smiled at LeRoy, a wide smile, full of healthy, large white teeth. For the first time, he looked familiar. He's got my smile, LeRoy thought, and then corrected himself. *I've* got *his* smile.

"Chris-tea-ann," LeRoy said.

"You got it," the old man said. "Now let's see if we can get your bag before they send it to Dallas, Texas."

From the baggage room, LeRoy followed his grandfather out of the terminal. They walked between the huge concrete pillars that held up a superhighway. It smelled bad, like the lobby and corridors of the housing project sometimes smelled, and LeRoy wasn't surprised to see a drunk, passed out and curled up beside one of the pillars.

"There's lots of sin and wickedness in New Orleans," the old man said. "Whiskey and women and worse. But I suppose you've seen your share of that, living where you have been."

LeRoy didn't like the sound of that. It was just his luck, he thought, that his grandfather would turn out to be a religious fanatic.

There was an old Chevrolet pickup parked two blocks away. It was battered and rusty, and there was a homemade wooden body sitting in the open bed of the truck. On the door was a homemade sign: A. CHAMBERS SHRIMP & CRABS.

"You wouldn't believe how much money they get to park your truck around here, boy," the old man said. "You better put that case up front. Smells of fish in the back."

It smelled of fish up front, too. The old man got behind the wheel and started the engine. He turned the headlights on, and drove out from under the superhighway. He drove down narrow streets for about a mile, then pulled up in front of a run-down building.

"What's this?" LeRoy asked.

"I figured you could probably use something to eat," the old man said. "This place does better than most."

"Can we get something to eat this late?"

"This is New Orleans, boy. People eat when they're hungry."

Inside it looked just about as old and run-down as it did outside. But it wasn't what LeRoy had expected. There were clean checkered tablecloths on the rickety tables, and the people inside, about half of them white, were well dressed. Whatever it was, it wasn't a saloon.

A waitress came to their table almost immediately. "Hello, Mr. Aaron," she said. She put water glasses in front of them, and a wicker basket holding something wrapped in a napkin.

"Mr. Alfred around?" the old man asked. He reached for the wicker basket, unfolded the napkin, and took out a large piece of French bread and a saucer stacked high with cubes of butter.

"Yes, sir," the waitress said. "I'll tell him you're here."

The old man pushed the wicker basket toward LeRoy. "You ever eat French bread before, boy?" he asked. "Try some."

It smelled delicious, and with some butter on it, LeRoy found it tasted as good as it smelled.

A large, fat black man wearing an apron walked up to the table. He had a bottle and three glasses in his hands. He set the glasses and the bottle on the table, then eased himself into a chair.

"I didn't expect to see you again tonight, Aaron," he said. "How old's he?"

"He's eighteen years, three months, and nine days," the old man said. "I figured that out on the way over here."

The fat man poured the contents of the bottle into the three glasses.

"*Santé,*" he said, raising his glass and taking a couple of healthy swallows.

"*Santé,*" the old man said, raising his glass and drinking. LeRoy took a swallow from his glass. It was wine, despite what the old man had said about sin and wickedness.

"*Santé* means 'To your good health' in French,

24

boy," the old man said. "Say hello to Mr. Alfred Davis, LeRoy."

"Pleased to meet you, boy," the fat man said. His grip on LeRoy's hand was firm and warm.

"LeRoy just got off the bus," the old man said. "I figured he could use something to eat. You got any red beans and rice left over? Maybe a piece of sausage?"

"If he's who I think he is, Aaron, I can do better than that. You ever eat any redfish, boy?"

"I don't think so," LeRoy said.

"You say 'sir' to your elders, boy," the old man said.

"He looks like his daddy, Aaron," the fat man said.

"We don't talk about his daddy, Alfred," said the old man. "You know that."

"Sorry," replied the other. He got up. "I'll go see about the redfish." He walked across the room and disappeared through a swinging door with the sign "Kitchen" on it.

"Alfred keeps a pretty good kitchen," the old man said.

"He knew my father?"

"Didn't you hear what I said about not talking about your father?" the old man asked. "Yeah, Alfred knew your daddy. Alfred and I go back a long time."

"Why don't we talk about my father?"

"Because he took off on your mother and you when you were little," the old man said. "That's why we don't talk about him."

"Maybe he had his reasons," LeRoy said.

"Maybe he did," the old man said. "But whatever they were, they're my reason for not talking about him. As far as I'm concerned, I don't have a son."

The redfish, which came to the table swimming in butter, was the best fish LeRoy had ever eaten. While he ate it, his grandfather was served, without having been asked, oysters on the half-shell. LeRoy had never seen a raw oyster before, and he couldn't understand how anybody could stick something that looked like that in his mouth. But his grandfather ate two large platefuls of them, washing them down with the wine.

Then, seeing that LeRoy was finished, he stood up.

"We better get going, boy," he said. "The night's half gone." He walked to the cash register and took out a thick wad of money. "What do I owe you?" he asked the waitress who had served him.

The question seemed to surprise her.

"Just a minute," she said, and walked quickly to the kitchen. Mr. Alfred came out.

"What's the matter with you, Aaron?" Mr. Alfred said. "Your money's no good in here. You know that."

"I like to pay my way," the old man said. He still had the money in his hand. LeRoy saw that the thick wad included three, maybe four, fifty-dollar bills. He could *see* that many. There were probably more.

"When I want your money, Aaron," Mr. Alfred said, "I'll ask for it."

"We're obliged," the old man said. "Aren't we, LeRoy?"

"That was a first-class meal, Mr. Alfred," LeRoy said. "Thank you."

"Come back again anytime, LeRoy," Mr. Alfred said. "Glad you liked it."

They went outside and got back into the truck. A few blocks away, the old man turned off one of the old and narrow streets onto a ramp. Ten seconds later, they were on a four-lane superhighway above the city.

The radio was playing. The old man snapped it off.

"Okay, boy, now you can tell me why you had to leave," the old man said. "Start at the beginning, and don't leave anything out."

LeRoy told his grandfather the whole story. The old man didn't say anything until he had finished. Then he said, "The world's full of sin and wickedness, boy. Everybody has to deal with it in his own way. If you need my help, all you have to do is ask."

"How could you help?" LeRoy asked, thinking out loud.

"Why, I could go back up there with you, for one thing, when you testify against those bums."

"I don't think I'm going up there until after the trial," LeRoy said.

The old man didn't say anything, but LeRoy sensed he hadn't liked that answer at all.

"You don't know people like that," LeRoy said. "They wouldn't think anything of cutting me."

"I've known my share of people who carried knives," the old man said. "The place for them is jail."

"I don't want to get cut," LeRoy said.

"Nobody wants to get cut," the old man said.

"But sometimes we got to take chances. I said I'd go with you, if you want."

At first, LeRoy thought the idea was pretty funny. This old man, taking on B.J. and Elton and Howard and the rest of the Wolves. But then it didn't seem so funny. There was something really tough about the old man. LeRoy realized that there was no way the old man would have let B.J. slice the buttons off his coat and then slash the jacket. He felt a little ashamed of the way he'd taken it.

"I wanted to get me a knife and do some cutting myself," he said.

"What you do when someone comes after you with a knife, boy," the old man said, "is protect yourself with an ax. And then you go for help to the law. That's what they're for."

"You just don't understand those guys," LeRoy said.

"I understand them," the old man said. "You don't." Then he changed the subject. "This is supposed to be one of the world's longest bridges," he said. "That water is Lake Pontchartrain."

LeRoy didn't reply. He couldn't think of anything to say. He could make out water and another bridge a mile or so away, but that was all he could see.

A few miles beyond the other side of the bridge, they turned to the left, and a few miles after that, he saw the sign: PASS CHRISTIAN.

"We're in Mississippi?" LeRoy asked.

"We're in Mississippi," the old man said. "Something wrong?"

"It's not what I expected," LeRoy said.

"How can you tell?" the old man replied. "Can't see nothing but the highway."

A few miles further down, they turned onto a two-lane road, and after another mile or so, onto a dirt road. Two hundred yards down the dirt road, they made a final turn and stopped. In the moonlight, LeRoy could see a wooden building, more like a shack, and behind it a lake or something. There was a pier heading into the water, and at the end of it, a funny-looking old boat, maybe thirty feet long.

The old man got out of the truck, grabbed LeRoy's suitcase, and started to walk toward the pier. LeRoy jumped out and followed him. They got on the boat. There was a cabin on the boat. The old man opened a door and turned on a light. "This is where you sleep," he said. "If you're going to be here, we'll have to start thinking about adding onto the house."

The cabin was about eight feet wide and twelve feet long. And it was jammed full of stuff, including three old deep freezers with rust showing through a half-dozen layers of paint. There was a little sink, a small, two-burner gas stove, and a tiny table. There was a tiny refrigerator and a bunk. The bunk was nothing more than a wooden shelf against the wall. But there were sheets and a blanket and a pillow on it, waiting for him.

"The head is through that door," the old man said.

"The what?"

"The toilet," the old man said. "You know how to work a marine toilet, LeRoy?" He didn't wait for an answer. "I expect not," the old man said. "Come on."

When he'd shown LeRoy the four steps you had

to go through to flush a marine toilet, the old man pointed to a switch on the cabin wall.

"When you're ready for bed," he said, "flick that. I'll see you in the morning."

"Good night," LeRoy said. Then he hesitated. "What would you like me to call you?"

"That's up to you, boy," the old man said. "You can call me sir, or you can call me granddaddy."

"How about grandfather?" LeRoy asked. Granddaddy was just too Southern.

"Grandfather would be fine, LeRoy," the old man said.

"Goodnight, Grandfather," LeRoy said. "And thanks."

"No thanks necessary," the old man replied, and then he left the cabin. LeRoy felt the boat rock as his grandfather jumped off onto the pier.

There was no way, LeRoy decided, that he was going to get any sleep at all. He wouldn't want the old man to know, but this was the first time he'd ever been on a boat. What if it sank? He was already aware that it was moving gently back and forth, sort of rocking.

But there was no sense sitting around in his clothes. He stripped to his underwear and got into the bunk. He pushed on the mattress. It was foam rubber, and very comfortable. He reached up and snapped off the light. He lay in the darkness, listening to the boat creak and the water splash up against the sides. And then he fell asleep.

He woke up suddenly, scared for some reason. The sun was out, and there were new sounds. There was a steady bub-bub-bub noise, and the smell of something like burning oil. He sat up on the bunk.

"Good morning," the old man said. "You were sleeping like a log."

LeRoy swung his feet out of the bunk and found his shoes. He slipped into them and stood up. The cabin door was open, and he walked through it. They weren't tied up at the pier anymore. There was nothing on that side of the boat but water. He went around to the back of the cabin. There was a flat wooden table out there. He walked around it. Far off, LeRoy could see a dark, barely visible line he realized was the shore.

Behind the boat, the water boiled up. There were steel poles sticking up from the floor of the boat, and from the end of the poles, what looked like wire ropes running into the water.

LeRoy went back into the cabin. The old man was sitting on a stool, one hand on a steering wheel.

"Where are we?" LeRoy asked. "What's going on?"

"Well, we're in the Mississippi Sound, boy," the old man said. "And what we're doing is dragging a net. That's how we earn our daily bread, LeRoy. We're shrimpers."

CHAPTER
4

"If you think you can handle this wheel, boy, keep us going straight. I'll fix us some breakfast."

"I can cook," LeRoy said.

"All right, then, you cook. We got about twenty minutes till we haul the net."

LeRoy opened the little refrigerator. There was a carton of eggs, a pound package of bacon, and a loaf of French bread.

"Bacon and eggs?" LeRoy asked. He could cook bacon and eggs.

"That's the idea," the old man said.

"How many pieces of bacon?" LeRoy asked.

"About half of what's there," the old man said. "And about four eggs."

"Four eggs and half a pound of bacon?" LeRoy replied.

"You better have the same boy," the old man

said. "You work up quite an appetite out here. You'll find out."

LeRoy made himself only two eggs, but the old man was right. He was able to eat a half-pound of bacon and half the loaf of French bread without any trouble at all.

When they were finished, the old man got up from the tiny table and motioned LeRoy to follow him outside. They went to the back of the boat. There was a small panel with several control levers on it.

"First thing you do, boy, is cut it down to idle," the old man said. He moved one of the levers. The bub-bub-bub sound of the engine changed pitch and LeRoy felt the boat slow down.

"Then you haul in the boards," the old man said. He pushed another lever, and there was a creaking sound. LeRoy saw that the cable at the end of the poles was being pulled in and wrapped around a drum. In about a minute, two pieces of wood, about six feet long and four feet wide, came out of the water and were hauled halfway up to the end of the poles

"Those are the boards, LeRoy," the old man told him. "When you drag them through the water, they keep the mouth of the net open." He pointed at the water. LeRoy could see the net, or at least the top of it. It looked like the net on the tennis court at the housing project before it had been all cut up.

"And then," the old man went on, pushing still another lever and causing another rope to start winding, "you pick up the bag of the net." The rest of the net came out of the water. LeRoy saw the bag. It was filled. The old man grabbed the rope and pulled the bag over the wooden table. Then he reached up and grasped a rope hanging from the bottom of the bag. He gave it a sharp jerk.

The contents of the bag spilled onto the table. Fish and shrimp and crabs poured out. The crabs scurried around the edges of the table, trying to get away. The fish flapped, trying to get air.

"My God!" LeRoy said.

"Don't blaspheme, boy," the old man said sharply. LeRoy looked at him. He was holding the net in his hands, tying the end again. "Then you put the whole thing back in the water," the old man said, pushing the net over the end of the boat and turning to the levers again. The net slipped back into the water, followed by the boards. "Finally, you run the engine up a little again," the old man finished, pushing the throttle lever. "And that's all there is to it. Except for picking the table, and heading the shrimp."

The old man bent over the table.

"I'll do the crabs," he said. "They'll get you unless you know what you're doing. You just watch what I do."

LeRoy was fascinated. The crabs sort of sat up on their hind legs and snapped their claws at the old man's hands as he went for them. But he was quicker than they were. He reached behind and grabbed them by the shell, throwing them into a five-gallon plastic paint bucket so fast LeRoy had trouble following him.

"Now, those ugly fish that look like little sharks, they're catfish," the old man said, when he'd finished the crabs. "They have barbs, one on each side and one on top. You get one of those barbs in you, leaves a nasty wound. But all you have to do is be careful." He started grabbing the catfish, using his thumbs and forefingers to quickly catch the barbs and throw them over the side of the boat. "You get the idea?"

"Yes, sir," LeRoy said. "I think so."

"Next haul, you can try it," the old man said. "This time, you just separate the trash fish from the shrimp. You're not afraid to get your hands in there, are you, boy?"

"No, sir," LeRoy said. He didn't like the idea of touching any of those live fish at all, but he would have died before admitting that to his grandfather. "But how do I tell a trash fish?"

"Anything that's not a shrimp is a trash fish," the old man said. He tugged at the end of the table by the side of the boat. It came loose in his hands, and he laid it on the floor. "Just slide the trash fish over the side," the old man said. "I'll go get us some ice."

LeRoy was glad the old man was gone. He wouldn't have wanted him to see the face he made the first time he reached for a shrimp and felt it move in his hands. He didn't like this at all. He had to remind himself that the old man did it all the time, and it hadn't hurt him any.

Within a couple of minutes, however, he had learned how to do it. He spread the mingled fish and shrimp with his fingers. Then he picked up the shrimp and dropped them into another five-gallon plastic paint bucket. He pushed the trash fish over the side.

And then, without warning, something bit him. He

jerked his hand off the table. There was a catfish, a miniature shark, stuck by the barb on his back to the ball of LeRoy's thumb.

He swore and shook his hand. The catfish went flying. He turned to find his grandfather smiling at him.

"I told you to be careful," the old man admonished. "Pinch the flesh where he got you and make it bleed. Otherwise it'll fester."

LeRoy did as he was told. He was aware that the old man was still looking at him, smiling at him. He gritted his teeth and finished picking the table.

"Not bad for your first time, boy," the old man said. "You'll get better."

They hauled the net four more times, for an hour each time, before quitting for the day. LeRoy got so that he could grab the catfish by their barbs and throw them over the side nearly as fast as the old man. But the crabs were too much for him.

"We'll get you a stout pair of leather gloves," the old man said. "And then we'll let you practice with those. Otherwise, they'll be calling you Three-Fingers LeRoy."

After the last haul, it took them about an hour to get back to St. Louis Bay from the Mississippi Sound. The old man showed him how to navigate by compass, and LeRoy steered while the old man beheaded the shrimp, squeezing them between his thumb and index finger. LeRoy realized that, sooner or later, he would have to do it, too. But the funny thing was, he didn't mind as much as he thought he should.

When they got to the mouth of St. Louis Bay, the old man stood beside him and showed him how to steer.

"Going upstream, LeRoy," he said, "in other words, away from the big water, you keep those red buoys on your right. It's as simple as that."

Ten minutes after they had passed through the mouth of St. Louis Bay, the old man pointed to the shore. "That's it, LeRoy," he said. "We're home." LeRoy could make out the pier, and a hundred yards from the pier, the wooden shack that was his grand-father's house. He steered the boat toward the pier. When they got close, the old man taught him, step by step, how to bring the boat alongside the pier. The old man went outside the cabin and tied up the boat. Then he came back and showed LeRoy how to shut off the engine.

"Well, that's how a fisherman makes his daily bread," the old man said. "What do you think?"

"I sort of liked it," LeRoy admitted. The old man winked at him.

"Well, come on," he said. "We got to take this stuff to New Orleans. It's way after noon." The old man pulled a battered, old-fashioned watch from his pocket. "Already quarter after one, as a matter of fact."

That's all? LeRoy thought. Quarter after one? It should be six, seven o'clock. We were out there for-ever.

"You go get the truck, boy," the old man sug-gested. "And back it up to the pier. I'll finish icing this stuff."

LeRoy just stood there, embarrassed.

"Can't drive, huh?" the old man asked. "Well, it's too late to teach you today, but maybe we'll find time tomorrow."

"We never had a car," LeRoy explained.

"Never be ashamed of something you can't control, boy," the old man said. "You start unloading the shrimp, and I'll go get the truck."

LeRoy took the plastic boxes filled with iced shrimp from the freezer and put them on the dock. The old man showed him how he plugged the freezers into an electric socket on the pier.

"Saves a lot of money, making your own ice," he said. "You wouldn't believe how much money they charge you for ice at the fish market, and how little they give you for your catch. That's why I make my own ice and sell my own catch in New Orleans."

When they had everything in the truck, the old man told him to get a change of clothes and bring them up to the "house." When he got there, LeRoy saw for the first time that the shack was built on maybe a fourth, even less, of a large concrete slab.

"Strip off your dirty clothes, underwear and all," the old man ordered, "and throw them in the washer. Don't worry about anybody seeing you naked. There's nobody out here but us. That's one of the nice things."

LeRoy was surprised to see that the washer-dryer was a new and expensive model, and that the shower was as fancy as any he'd seen anywhere, even on TV. He thought about the shack and the concrete slab, and when he'd finished his shower, he asked the old man, "Where'd that slab come from?"

"I poured that slab, that's where it came from," the old man said. "Used to be a house on it. And I built that, too."

"What happened to it?"

"Hurricane Camille got it," the old man said. "Almost got me, too. Put that old boat two hundred yards inland. Had a terrible time getting it back in the water."

"Why didn't you rebuild the house? No insurance?"

"Why rebuild it?" the old man replied softly. "I mean the way it was. Your grandmomma had gone to her reward. You and your momma was up North. I built just enough for me."

LeRoy looked at him without saying anything.

"The thing is, boy," the old man went on, "I figured that you'd sell it, and I just didn't have the heart to build a house for strangers."

"What do you mean, I'd sell it?"

"When the good Lord calls me, boy, you'll get all this. You're my only kin. I didn't think you'd want it."

"But it's beautiful here!" LeRoy said. "Why would I want to sell this place?"

"Well, for one thing," the old man said, "until last night, you never saw it." Then he closed the conversation. "Come on, boy, there's a mess of people in New Orleans already thinking about eating the shrimp and crab we're going to take them."

On the way into New Orleans, LeRoy was willing to believe that the bridge across Lake Pontchartrain was the longest one in the world. He couldn't see from one end of it to the other. He wondered what would happen if the old truck broke down. It was a long way to the nearest service station. Much too far to walk.

"What happens if we get a flat or something?" he asked. "Or if the engine stops?"

"If we get a flat, we change tires," the old man said. LeRoy knew the old man thought it was a dumb question.

"And if something goes wrong with the engine, then what?"

"Then we fix it," the old man said. "It don't happen often. I take care of my equipment. You take care of your machines, and they'll take care of you, boy."

"But what if it just breaks?" LeRoy insisted. "And you can't fix it? Then what?"

"Open the glove compartment," the old man said. LeRoy opened it. There was a radio inside, and a microphone. "That's what they call a CB," the old man said. "You get on the CB, on channel 9, and you tell 'em you're in trouble."

He looked at LeRoy. "Go on," he said. "Turn it on."

When LeRoy hesitated, the old man reached over and turned on the radio. "Got forty channels on that," he said. "Don't know why. I never use but two." He moved a switch. There was a hissing noise. "Channel 9's the emergency channel," the old man said. "Channel 19's the truckers' channel. Truckers and people on the highway."

He picked up the microphone. "Breaker nineteen for a radio check," he said. "Come back to the Old Fisherman."

Almost immediately, there was a reply. "Got you loud and strong, Old Fisherman," a voice came over the radio. "What's your ten-twenty? Come back to the Kansas Kid."

The old man handed LeRoy the microphone.

"Tell him we're westbound, halfway across the big bridge," he said. LeRoy hesitated. "Go on, push that button and tell him," the old man said.

LeRoy was uncomfortable, embarrassed.

"Go on, tell him," the old man insisted.

LeRoy pushed the button. "We're halfway across the bridge," he said.

"You're supposed to tell him which way you're going and to come back," the old man said.

"Old Fisherman," the radio said, "the Kansas Kid is headed east on the bridge, about halfway. What are you rolling in? Come back."

The old man took the microphone from LeRoy. "The Old Fisherman's in a westbound country Cadillac," the old man said. "Read you loud and clear, Kansas Kid. Come back."

"Old Fisherman," the radio said, "got my eyeballs on you."

A blue Buick, a new one, pulled abreast of the truck. The driver played "Shave and a haircut, two bits" on his horn, and waved as he passed. LeRoy saw the Kansas license plate.

"Have a good day, Kansas Kid," the old man said. "This is the Old Fisherman clear."

"Same to you, Old Fisherman," the radio said. "This is the Kansas Kid, with the pedal to the metal, clear to the Old Fisherman."

The old man smiled. He reached over to put the microphone back in the glove compartment.

"You trying to tell me that white dude would have stopped if we broke down?" LeRoy asked.

"Oh, I think he would have stopped all right," the old man said. "Don't know how much help he would have been. I've generally found that the fancier the car, the less people know about what makes it run."

"You really think he would have stopped?" LeRoy asked. He found that hard to believe.

"You put one of these CBs in your car," the old man said, "you sort of make an agreement to help people who need help. Most people live up to it."

"You break down where I live," LeRoy said, "and you call for help, some dude would come and steal your shrimp, that's what would happen."

"Well, it's not that way down here," the old man said firmly. "And I don't know if it's true where you come from, either. Even if you don't think so right now, boy, there's more good people than the other kind."

That's what you think, old man, LeRoy thought. But he didn't say it out loud.

CHAPTER
5

They made seven stops in New Orleans. At each stop, the same thing happened. The old man took shrimp and crabs into the kitchen of a restaurant. The shrimp were weighed and the crabs counted, and he was paid in cash. No one tried to argue about the price, and no one said he couldn't use that many shrimp, or that many crabs. They took what the old man offered, and they paid for it.

It hadn't been that way in the Del Monte Cafeteria. The chefs there had spent most of their mornings fighting with the vendors. Most of LeRoy's experience had been with the vegetable vendors, but he'd heard the fights between the chefs and the chicken vendors, the meat vendors, and the fish and oyster vendors.

As far as the vendors were concerned, everything they tried to deliver was first-rate, underpriced, and

43

an all-round bargain. As far as the cooks were concerned, it was right on the edge of spoiling, overpriced, and, anyhow, they didn't need it.

"Is it always like that?" LeRoy asked.

"Like what?"

"You tell them how much they can have, and how much it is, and they don't even fight with you?"

"What do you know about food?" the old man asked.

"I was working in a cafeteria," LeRoy said.

"Doing what?"

"Making salads."

"I didn't know that," the old man said. "I had the idea you were mopping floors, washing dishes, things like that."

"I started out washing dishes," LeRoy said.

"You like working in a kitchen?" the old man asked. "You like cooking?"

"It's all right, I guess."

"We have some of the best restaurants in the world down here," the old man said proudly.

"We got some pretty good ones where I come from, too," LeRoy said.

"The best ones are here," the old man insisted. "Anybody who knows about food will tell you that."

LeRoy had to bite his lip to keep from smiling at the old man. He didn't bite it in time. The old man saw him smile.

"If you think that's funny, boy, you just don't know about food," the old man said.

"You know what my boss told me one time?" LeRoy replied. "And he was the *head* chef."

"Couldn't have been much of a chef if he worked

in a cafeteria," the old man said. "Cafeterias are nearly as bad as those places that fry frozen Argentine ground beef and call them hamburgers."

"Huh?"

"On a soft-bread roll," the old man said, warming to the subject. "With a sweet pickle slice, catsup, and some yellow stuff that's supposed to be mustard."

LeRoy understood that the old man was talking about a hamburger joint, one of the chains.

"I went in one, one time," the old man went on. "They actually gave me one of those things they call hamburgers with Thousand Island dressing on it. Enough to make anybody who knows anything about food throw up, that's what it was."

That was too much. LeRoy had to laugh.

"I don't suppose you liked the French fries, either?" he asked.

"About as big around as a pencil," the old man said. "I don't know what those potatoes really are, but they're not *pommes frites*, I know that."

"They're not what?"

"Pommes frites," the old man said. "That's French for fried potatoes. *French*-fried potatoes."

LeRoy was still smiling, right on the edge of laughing out loud, and the old man saw it.

"I was going to take you to a place and show you what a good cook can do with the shrimp we caught this morning," the old man said. "But now you're going to eat a *proper* hamburger, with some *proper* French fries, whether you like it or not."

They drove to a part of town LeRoy had never seen before. And he'd never seen anything like it, either. The streets were narrow, and all the buildings seemed to be about two hundred years old. They had balconies built out over the sidewalk, held up by what looked like cast-iron pipes.

"This is what they call the French Quarter," the old man said. "The *Vieux Carré*," he went on. "That means 'old quarter' in French."

"We would have torn all these old buildings down where I come from," LeRoy said.

"I don't doubt that at all, boy," the old man said. "And built one of those housing developments you lived in, right?"

"There's a lot wrong with housing developments," LeRoy said. "But at least they're not going to fall down from old age." As he said it, he saw in his mind's eye the steel door to his apartment after the Wolves had beat it in with a fire extinguisher.

"Some of these buildings have been standing since before there was a Chicago," the old man said. "I expect that they're not going to fall down any time soon."

"You mean that?" LeRoy asked. "You mean they're really that old?"

"Yes, they are," the old man said. "And I'll tell you something else. I saw a story in the newspaper that said this is the most expensive real estate in the country. What that means is a lot of people with a lot more money than you have think this is a pretty good place to live."

LeRoy wasn't sure if the old man was just saying that, or if it was true. But he didn't have a chance to find out, for the old man suddenly stopped the truck and backed into a parking space.

He handed LeRoy the last of the shrimp coolers, and picked up the last five-gallon paint bucket full of crabs. LeRoy followed him down the street and around a corner, and then down a narrow alley. He stopped in front of a steel door and pushed a button. In a moment, the door was opened. A black man in cook's whites, including a foot-tall, stiffly starched white hat, smiled and waved them inside.

"Ça va, mon vieux?" he said.

"Bon, et tu?" the old man replied. LeRoy didn't know what they said, but it was obviously some foreign language, and the old man apparently could speak it. "Louis, this is my grandson," he added.

"How are you, boy?" the chef said. He put out his hand and gave LeRoy a big smile.

"What was that you were talking?" LeRoy asked.

"Why, I guess you could say it was French," the chef said. "But what it really was, was pure, 100 percent Cajun, wasn't it, Aaron?"

He took the crabs from the old man and carried them to one of the stoves. A huge stock pot was sitting, steaming, on the stove. He up-ended the five-gallon paint bucket full of crabs into it, and looked at his watch. Then he took the shrimp from LeRoy and set them on a wooden work table.

"Tony!" he called, and a young man, a white dude about LeRoy's age, walked over. "Have at it," Louis said. "And while you're shelling, put the large ones in one bowl, the mediums in another, and the small ones in a third."

The young man nodded. LeRoy knew who he was. He was low man in the kitchen, the guy who did the dirty jobs. LeRoy had been the low man for a while in the Del Monte kitchen.

"LeRoy was working in a kitchen in Chicago," the old man said.

47

"That so? What were you doing?"

"Salads," LeRoy said.

"You ever do any frying?" Louis asked.

"You mean eggs and hamburgers and things like that?" LeRoy asked.

"No," the old man answered for Louis, laughing. "He don't mean eggs and hamburgers. He means *frying*."

"I'm looking for a good fry cook," the chef said.

"LeRoy don't know a whole lot about good food, Louis," the old man said. "I thought I'd ask you to sauté us some of them shrimp, but LeRoy says he'd rather have a hamburger."

LeRoy gave the old man a dirty look. If the old man noticed, it didn't show.

"Nothing wrong with a hamburger," Louis said. "But you want some shrimp, Aaron?"

"I'd be obliged," the old man said.

"Go on out in the dining room," Louis said. "And I'll have the girl bring you a glass of wine."

The dining room was a lot fancier than LeRoy had expected, considering how old and run-down the building looked. But then he remembered the kitchen was also fancy. It had a lot of sophisticated, expensive cooking equipment.

They sat down at a table near the kitchen. It was only about five o'clock, but already the restaurant was filling up. Just as soon as they'd sat down, a waitress came to the table and put ice water in front of them.

"You going to need a menu, Mr. Aaron?" she asked. "Or is the boss taking care of you?"

"He's taking care of us, thank you," the old man said.

48

"I'd like to see a menu," LeRoy said. "Just to look at one."

"Sure," the waitress said, and handed him a menu. LeRoy opened it, and looked first at what they were serving, then at the prices. He didn't believe his eyes.

"Are these prices for real?" he asked.

The waitress was already back at their table, with a basket of French bread, a platter of butter, and two glasses of wine. She heard what LeRoy asked, and smiled at him.

"They're for real," she said.

"You get a reputation for serving really good food in a town where almost all food is better than most other places," the old man said, "and you can charge practically anything you want to charge. People who don't like the prices can go to a cafeteria."

LeRoy had to smile. He shook his head. The old man went on. "Not only are we getting what you call a professional discount, but we're taking it out in trade. You're going to pay for your hamburger with some of the shrimp you helped catch this morning." He picked up his wine glass, and when LeRoy had raised his, the old man clicked glasses. *"Santé,"* he said.

"Santé," LeRoy replied. He thought that was kind of fun. "What's a Cajun?" he asked.

"You ever read that poem, *Evangeline*, by Henry Wadsworth Longfellow?" the old man asked.

"No," LeRoy answered.

"Well, it tells the story of how the English ran some French out of Acadia — Nova Scotia — when they took over Canada, a long time ago. They just told them to pack up and get out. A lot of them came down here. Sad story. Anyway, some of the people already here — English, Indians, black people, even some Germans — couldn't speak French. *Acadians* came out, after a while, sounding like *Cajuns*. Then when they started to marry each other, they called themselves that. Cajuns. You're part Cajun."

"What do you mean by that?"

"Just what I said. You're part Cajun. My momma spoke it better than she spoke English. And her poppa, he couldn't hardly speak English at all."

"You're telling me I'm part white?" LeRoy asked.

"I didn't say that," the old man said. "I said you were part Cajun. That means, on my side, you got some French in you, and some Indian, and for all I know, some German, too. I don't know nothing about what you got from your mother."

"And you speak it?"

"I speak it," the old man said. "And after you're down here a while, you'll learn how yourself."

The waitress delivered their food before LeRoy could ask any more questions. She gave the old man a plate something like a soup bowl. In it were maybe eight huge shrimp, a few mushrooms, peas, and some French-fried potatoes. The fries were as big around as LeRoy's thumb, and cut in squares.

"They call this Shrimp Richelieu," the old man said. "Richelieu was a cardinal in France."

LeRoy looked at his plate. On it was, he supposed, a hamburger, because it was fried ground beef. But that was the only thing it had in common with what LeRoy thought of as a hamburger. The "hamburger" was about half an inch thick. Instead of being round, it was oblong, longer than it was wide. It had been shaped to fit an oblong hard-crusted roll. The top of the roll was on one side of the plate. There was also a thick slice of tomato sitting on some lettuce, a large slice of pickle, and a dozen French-fried potatoes. There was no way, LeRoy thought, that it was going to fit in his mouth after he put the tomato and the lettuce on the hamburger, and then added the top of the hard-crusted roll.

The waitress set a mustard jar on the table.

"Can I have some catsup?" LeRoy asked.

"No, you can't," the old man said flatly. "And before you start slopping that mustard on the meat, you better taste it. That's *real* mustard."

LeRoy tasted the mustard. A little drop of it on the end of his tongue almost burned.

"That's hot!" he said.

"That's proper mustard," the old man said. "Just spread a little bit on the meat."

LeRoy did that, and then started to put the lettuce and the tomato on top.

"Just leave that where it is," the old man said. "And eat it with a knife and fork. And eat the hamburger that way, too. Your mouth isn't that big."

LeRoy cut a piece of the hamburger and the roll underneath with his knife and fork and put it in his mouth. The hamburger was still pink inside, and the juices had soaked into the roll. The mustard made it taste different. "That isn't really a hamburger," he said. "That's a hamburger steak."

"No, it isn't, either," the old man insisted. "A hamburger steak's about twice that big. What that is, LeRoy, is a *proper* hamburger."

"It's delicious," LeRoy said.

51

"Finish chewing what you've got in your mouth," the old man said. "Then take a swallow of wine, and I'll give you a taste of my shrimp."

The old man speared one of his shrimp on a fork and handed it to LeRoy. LeRoy bit into it. It was crisp and sweet. He hadn't eaten many shrimp before, but this was the best shrimp he had ever eaten.

"That's good," he said. "Was that one we caught this morning?"

The old man nodded. "You can't get shrimp like that in Chicago," he said, "if you have all the money in the world. About eight hours ago, that shrimp was in the Gulf of Mexico. The fresher they are, the better they taste."

"You always eat this way down here?"

"We try to," the old man said, smiling at him. "We're so busy eating we don't have time to tear down our falling-down buildings. 'Course, if you don't like it, I know a place about three blocks away where they serve the kind of hamburgers you're used to."

"This is just fine, thank you," LeRoy said.

"Well, maybe there's hope for you yet," the old man said.

CHAPTER
6

The next morning, LeRoy woke up when the old man came on board the shrimp boat. He climbed out of his bunk and went on deck to help the old man untie the lines that held the boat to the pier. It was still dark, but LeRoy could see once his eyes grew accustomed to it.

The buoys marking the channel had flashing lights on them. The old man showed LeRoy how to steer between them to get out into the Mississippi Sound. Then the sun came up. The water was so smooth and slick it looked oily. There was something very beautiful about the whole thing. Even the air smelled good.

The shrimp were running. Whenever they pulled the net, the bag was heavy with shrimp and crabs.

"Don't get the idea," the old man said as they were separating the shrimp and crabs from the trash fish, "that it's always this way. Sometimes, when you pull the net, all you get is trash fish. Or jellyfish. And every once in a while, a water-soaked log or an old automobile tire."

"Beginner's luck?" LeRoy asked.

"Something like that, maybe," the old man replied. "But I'm glad we're getting a good, fast haul today."

"Why?"

"Well, it'll give us a chance to run by the courthouse and get you a learner's permit, for one thing," the old man said. "And if there's still time, I want to stop by the lumberyard, too. We'll do without a fancy meal in New Orleans, and make supper ourselves when we get home."

They came off the water just before eleven. By half-past three, they were through with their deliveries in New Orleans, and back in Mississippi. But the old man didn't turn off the interstate highway where he normally did. He drove another ten miles down, and turned off at the Biloxi exit.

There was a short line of people at the driver's license bureau. LeRoy saw that the state troopers were in charge of issuing driver's licenses and learner's permits. Seeing the police reminded LeRoy of the skinny housing development cop and the junkie.

A cop headed right for them, a great big-bellied white man in a two-tone brown uniform. "It's about time you got yourself a license, Mr. Chambers," he said to the old man.

"Hello, Ellwood," the old man said. "You're putting on a little around the waist, I see." They shook hands like old friends. The cop looked at LeRoy.

"This must be Les's boy," he said.

"This is my grandson," the old man said. "Boy, say hello to Sheriff Greenhaw."

The big cop, the sheriff, shook LeRoy's hand.

"LeRoy, isn't it?" he asked.

"That's right," LeRoy said.

"He was raised a Yankee, Ellwood," the old man said. "He don't know he's supposed to say 'Yes, sir' to his elders."

"How's your daddy, LeRoy?" the sheriff asked. Then he made a face. "I'm sorry," he said. "That was dumb of me. The thing is, LeRoy, I grew up with your daddy."

"No offense taken, Ellwood," the old man said.

The line had moved up. They were now in front of the desk.

"Learner's permit?" the highway patrolman asked.

"Please," the old man said.

"You got your birth certificate, son?" the highway patrolman asked.

"No, we don't have it," the old man said. "I forgot about that."

The highway patrolman shrugged his shoulders.

"I remember when LeRoy was born," the sheriff said. "His daddy called me long distance from Chicago to tell me. That was eighteen years and some months ago. He's old enough."

"The law says 'a birth certificate,' Sheriff," the highway patrolman said.

"It says 'a birth certificate or other satisfactory proof of age.' You just consider me satisfactory proof," the sheriff said.

"I guess that would be all right," the highway patrolman agreed. "Just fill this out," he told LeRoy, handing him a form.

"You going to be staying with your grandfather, LeRoy?" the sheriff asked.

"Yes, sir," LeRoy said.

"If I can ever do anything for you, you just yell, hear?"

"Thank you," LeRoy said.

"Good to see you, Mr. Chambers," the sheriff said, and shook the old man's hand again.

"You give my respects to your daddy," the old man said.

"Yes, sir," the sheriff said, "I'll surely do that." He patted the old man on the shoulder, smiled, and walked away.

They drove back to Pass Christian along the Gulf Highway. There were a number of motels and hotels, all of which looked expensive, and miles and miles of white sand beaches. They passed a building surrounded by a white painted fence. LeRoy looked at it curiously. There were three flags flying in front of the house—an American flag, and what looked like two Confederate flags. And then he saw the sign:

BEAU REVOIR. THE LAST HOME OF
JEFFERSON DAVIS,
President of the Confederacy.

LeRoy felt himself getting mad. "What's that, anyway?" he asked.

"That's where Jefferson Davis passed his last days," the old man said.

"It looks like some kind of *memorial*," LeRoy said.

"That's what it is," the old man said. "A memorial and a museum. We get some free time, I'll take you through it. All kinds of interesting old things in there."

"They should have burned it to the ground," LeRoy said angrily.

The old man laughed.

"If old Matthew Chambers had heard you say that," he said, "he'd have taken a horsewhip to you."

"Who?"

"Matthew Chambers. He thought Jefferson Davis was about as good a man as they come. He was in the honor guard when they buried him."

"Who was he? Did he — did he own us when we were slaves?"

"Not hardly," the old man said. "He was a master sailmaker in the Confederate navy. Sailed on the *Alabama* with Admiral Semmes. I remember him well, from when I was a little boy. He lived to be a hundred and one. Died in the Veterans' Hospital right here in Biloxi."

"With the same name as ours? What about that?"

"He had the same name as we do because he was my grandfather," the old man said.

"A white man?" LeRoy asked. That was the only explanation he could think of.

"A little darker than you," the old man said. "He was what they called a free man of color. I used to have pictures of him. They got lost in Hurricane Camille. But there's pictures of him in the County Historical Society, and in the library in Jackson."

"You're telling me my great-grandfather —"

"He would be your great-great-grandfather," the old man corrected him.

"He fought for the *Confederacy?*"

"Indeed he did," the old man said. "Got a couple of medals, too."

"And you think that was right?"

"He thought it was right," the old man said. "Otherwise, he wouldn't have done it. I told you, he was a free man of color."

"What did he do after they lost the war?"

"He went back to sea, and then after he got too old for that, he worked in a sail loft here in Biloxi. We Chamberses have been going to sea for a long time, LeRoy," the old man said, and there was pride in his voice.

"You call going out there in that dinky little boat going to *sea?*" LeRoy asked, pointing to the smooth Gulf of Mexico. He was sorry the minute he said it. But the old man had made him mad. The last thing he'd needed to hear was that one of his ancestors had fought for the Confederacy. Then he realized that wasn't really what had upset him. It was that the old man seemed to have all the answers, and that he had none. The old man made him feel stupid.

And now the old man did it again. He laughed out loud.

"You know what you are, LeRoy?" he said. "You're what they call an instant expert. You been shrimping *twice*, so you know all there is to know about the Gulf of Mexico. Well, just to set you straight, boy, that smooth lake out there got all riled up a couple of years ago, and before it smoothed out again, it came through here and killed two hundred people and did three hundred million dollars worth of damage."

LeRoy gave the old man a dirty look. The old man just kept on smiling.

When they got to the dirt road that led to his shack and boat, the old man pulled to the side of the road and stopped. He opened the door and climbed out.

"Slide over," he said to LeRoy. "If you're going to learn to drive, this is as good a place as any to start."

It wasn't the first truck LeRoy had ever been in. He knew all about the clutch, brake, and gas pedals. It was just that he had never had a chance to really drive. When he slid behind the wheel, he pushed the clutch pedal to the floor and moved the gearshift lever into and out of gear.

"You seem to know what you're doing," the old man said, when he got in beside him. "Do you?"

"Maybe you better explain the gears to me," LeRoy said.

"Standard H," the old man said. LeRoy knew no more about that than he did about sailmaking. But the old man saved him the embarrassment of having to admit it. " Reverse is in the upper left-hand corner," he said. "First gear is below. Second is in the upper right-hand, and high in the lower right-hand."

LeRoy pulled the gearshift lever into low gear, let out on the clutch, and stepped on the gas. The truck moved off far more smoothly than LeRoy had expected. He shifted into second and then into high.

"Well, maybe there's hope for you yet," the old

man said. "You get a little more practice, and we'll see about getting you a license."

LeRoy looked over at the old man. The old man was smiling just the way he had been when he'd called LeRoy an instant expert.

LeRoy smiled back.

"When you get to the house, try not to drive into the bay," the old man said.

LeRoy managed to stop the truck smoothly, and just about where he wanted to stop.

"If you want, you can practice a little," the old man said. "I wouldn't go on the paved road just yet, if I were you. But I can't see how you could do a whole lot of damage going back and forth on the dirt one. Practice turning around."

"By myself?"

"I got some measuring to do," the old man said, getting out of the truck and slamming the door shut.

LeRoy spent the next hour driving back and forth on the dirt road. The first couple of times he turned around were difficult, but pretty soon he could do even that without much trouble. Whenever he got near the house, he saw the old man either measuring something or sitting with his legs hanging over the edge of the concrete slab, writing on a clipboard.

Finally, on one of LeRoy's back-and-forth trips, the old man waved him over. LeRoy stopped the truck and the old man got back in.

"Take us into town," he said. "I want to stop by the lumberyard."

"You want me to drive into town?" LeRoy asked.

"You're not going to be much help to me if all

60

you can do is go up and down a dirt road," the old man replied.

It was five miles to town. LeRoy was nervous the first time a car came toward them, heading in the other direction, but by the time they reached the lumberyard, he was almost confident. Driving wasn't all that special, when you got right down to it.

Still, he was glad to find the lumberyard on their side of Pass Christian, rather than in the town itself, or on the other side of town. After he got a little more practice, of course, it would be different, but right now he would just as soon not drive through town.

He followed the old man into the lumberyard office.

The proprietor looked very much like the old man, except that he was white. He was built like a barrel, had a full set of white teeth, and looked as if he ate pretty well.

"What can I do for you, Aaron?" he asked.

"If the price is right, Jesse," the old man said, "I might be talked into taking some wormy wood off your hands."

"You finally going to rebuild your place?" the proprietor asked, shaking the old man's hand.

"Got to," the old man said. "My grandson came home. Can't keep him living on the boat forever."

"My God," the man said. "This is Lester's boy? He's near a man. Are we getting that old?" He put out his hand, and when LeRoy gave his to him, he shook it so hard it hurt. LeRoy decided that the man naturally shook hands that way, because he was so strong, and wasn't showing off.

"You are," the old man said. "I'm not."

"You got some idea of what you're going to do?" the proprietor asked the old man.

"No," the old man said. "I thought I'd just start nailing one board to another and see how it comes out." He handed a sheet of paper to the man.

"Ask a dumb question, get a dumb answer," the proprietor said. He went quickly over the list. "You want this all at once, Aaron?"

"I'd be obliged to have the framing material tomorrow," the old man said. "The roofing and other stuff can wait a couple of days."

"This looks like enough to finish the whole place," the man remarked.

"I figure it is," the old man said. "If you're going to do something, you might as well go whole hog."

"Aaron, you probably could save a few dollars if you went to that place in Slidell and had them precut the whole thing for you."

"I'll do my own work, thank you. That way, I won't hide a knothole by accident, or forget to drive as many nails as I need."

The proprietor chuckled. "Okay. I'll have all the framing lumber delivered in the morning."

"I'd be obliged, Jesse," the old man said, and they shook hands again.

The proprietor extended his hand to LeRoy. "Nice to meet you, boy," he said.

LeRoy was barely able to keep his temper under control. He did not like being called "boy" by a white man. The old man must have seen something in his face, for when they were back in the truck, he asked, "Now what's bothering you?"

"I don't like being called 'boy,' " LeRoy said.

"Oh, is that what it is?"

"That's what it is."

"You think he's calling you 'boy' because you're black?" the old man asked. But he didn't wait for an answer. "He called you 'boy' because you're not quite a man. Get the chip off your shoulder, boy."

"You sure seem to get along pretty well with the white people," LeRoy said.

"I get along pretty well with most people," the old man said. "But if you're talking about Jesse Hamm in particular, I do get along with him pretty special."

"How come?"

"The way you tell who your friends are, boy," the old man said, "is by what they do for you when you're in trouble."

"What do you mean by that?"

"When Hurricane Camille came through here, and got the house, and put the boat three hundred yards out of the water, they evacuated me up near Jackson. When I got back here, Jesse had a bulldozer and a crew already at work to get that boat back in the water."

"What's so special about that?" LeRoy asked.

"Well, the hurricane got his lumberyard and his house, too. But he put his bulldozer to work getting my boat in the water because he knew that unless that boat got back in the water, it was going to be ruined. And if it was ruined, I wouldn't have a way to make my living."

"He got paid for it, didn't he?" LeRoy replied.

"No," the old man said. "He didn't. Not as much as it was worth, anyway. He let me pay for the diesel fuel, and the crew wages, just so it wouldn't look like charity, but he wouldn't take a dime for the use of the dozer. And anybody with a working dozer after the hurricane came through could ask whatever he wanted for the rent of it."

CHAPTER
7

Wen they had come back off the water the next day and loaded their catch in the truck, the old man asked, "You ever work any with wood?"

"No," LeRoy confessed. He had seen, as he helped unload the catch, a pile of lumber stacked on the slab, covered with a gray plastic sheet.

"You don't drive well enough, and you don't have a license, so you can't go into New Orleans by yourself," the old man said. "But there's no reason both of us have to go. And somebody's got to cut those two-by-fours."

LeRoy had a mental picture of himself with a hand saw. But the old man went into the shack and came back with an electric circular saw and a long, heavy-duty extension cord.

"Pull that plastic sheet off the lumber," he ordered. "And weight it down somehow so it won't blow away." Then he went back into the shack and returned with a tape measure, a flat pencil, and a piece of metal in the shape of an L, two feet tall and a foot across.

The old man pulled one of the long two-by-fours from the stack and laid it over the edge of the concrete slab.

"Watch what I do," he said. He held up the L-shaped piece of metal. "This is what you call a square," he said. "You put it up against the wood this way. And then you take this pencil — "

"That's a funny-looking pencil," LeRoy said. He was starting to smile.

"Flat pencils don't roll away from you," the old man said. "Then you mark the line."

"I got it that far." LeRoy was smiling, just a little sarcastically.

"If you look close," the old man said, "you'll see some black stuff in the middle of the pencil. You mark with that."

"Got it," LeRoy said. "What do they call that black stuff?"

"They call it lead. But it's not lead. Ever try writing with a tire weight?"

They were chuckling now, both of them.

"Thank Edison," the old man said.

"Huh?" LeRoy said.

"I say that every time I pick up one of these electric saws," the old man said. "I've sawed more wood than I like to remember with a hand saw." He turned on the saw, and cut through one of the two-by-fours about an inch from the end.

"You put that first mark as close to the edge as you can," he explained, "but far enough in so you

66

cut off the splits in the end. You see?" He held out the piece he had cut off. LeRoy could see where it was split.

"Then you take the tape," the old man continued, "and you measure off ninety-six inches. That's exactly eight feet. You take the pencil and the square and you mark it. Then you cut it off. Am I going too fast for you?"

"I think I could handle that all right," LeRoy said.

"The important thing to remember is not to put your fingers where the saw's going to cut. That way you won't get blood all over my saw."

"I'll try to keep that in mind," LeRoy said. "How many pieces of wood am I supposed to cut?"

"We'll need 120, 130 of them. Can you count that high?"

"If I use my fingers *and* my toes," LeRoy said.

"Okay, then," the old man said. "I'll leave you to it, and go to New Orleans to get us some eating money. What would you like for supper?"

"How about a steak?" LeRoy said. "About that thick?" He held up his fingers, two inches apart.

"You're a carpenter's *helper,* boy," the old man said. "You work your way up to thick steaks."

"In that case, why don't you get a pizza?" LeRoy asked.

"I'll think on it," the old man said. He got into the truck and drove off.

LeRoy started cutting the two-by-fours to size. He was a little afraid of the saw at first. The way it ripped through the wood was frightening. He was very careful with it, even after he'd grown used to it.

The first couple of two-by-fours he cut to size, he did one at a time. Then he realized it would be a lot easier to line up five or six of them and cut off the short ends all at once, measure them at once, and then cut off the other ends.

He had cut about thirty two-by-fours when he heard the telephone ring. At first he wasn't sure what it was. For one thing, the sound of the circular saw had made his ears ring. And for another, it was a strange kind of a telephone ring. But after he'd listened to the buzzing ring a couple of times, he knew what it was. He went into the shack.

He'd been in the shack only once, the day before, to put his dirty clothes in the washer-dryer, and he hadn't really looked around much. He found the telephone by listening to the ringing. It was on the floor, under the old man's bed. The bed was an old-time brass bed. When LeRoy sat on it, just before he picked up the telephone, he wondered if it had gone through that hurricane the old man was always talking about.

"Hello?"

"Mr. Chambers?" a woman's voice asked.

"Mr. Chambers isn't here right now," LeRoy said.

"LeRoy? LeRoy? Is that you, honey?"

"Hey, Momma," LeRoy said, feeling his throat get all tight.

"How are you, honey?" his mother asked.

"I'm fine," LeRoy said. "The old man had me out this morning, pulling shrimp and crabs out of the ocean, and now he's got me building a house. Aside from that, I'm just fine."

"I wanted to tell you I've got a place to live," she

said cheerfully. "I took a furnished room. It's all I really need."

LeRoy remembered the slashed-open furniture. He didn't like having his mother in a furnished room, but at least she was safe there.

"The police were by to see me," she said. "That white one looks like a bum."

"The junkie," LeRoy said. "What did he want?"

"He just wanted to know if you were all right."

"You tell him I was down here?"

"No."

"Don't tell them, unless you have to. Tell them I run off, and you don't know where I am."

She didn't reply to that.

"How are you getting along with your grandfather? Do you like it down there?"

"He's a nice old guy," LeRoy heard himself say. "A little strange. He lives in a shack."

"What do you mean, a shack? He had a house, a beautiful house. Your father used to show me pictures of it. It was right on the water."

"It got wiped out by a hurricane," LeRoy said. "What he lives in now is a shack."

"Is there room for both of you?"

"I sleep on the boat," LeRoy said. And then he realized that what he thought was kind of funny would probably make his mother worry. "No problem, Momma. And, boy, do we eat good."

"Just as soon as I can, I'll send you a little money.'"

"Don't worry about that, Momma. The old man's got a roll of fifty-dollar bills you'd have to see to believe."

"Can you find some kind of work down there?"

"You haven't been listening to me, Momma," LeRoy said. "From five o'clock in the morning until lunchtime, I'm a fisherman — if that's what you call somebody who goes out and drags for shrimp. And from lunchtime on, I'm a carpenter's helper."

"For who?" she asked.

"For the old man," he said. "It's not bad down here, Momma. The weather's nice. You ought to think about coming down."

"What would I do in Mississippi?" she asked.

"Well, I'm not coming to Chicago anytime soon," he said. "Not until the thing with the Wolves dies down."

"Please deposit another $2.35 for an additional three minutes," the operator's voice said.

"I'll call again in a couple of days, baby," Le-Roy's mother said. "Bye, honey."

The phone went dead in his ear before he could say good-bye.

He hung it up, and then looked around the room. The old man was living pretty simply. The bathroom was fancy, and there was everything he needed in the kitchen, but there wasn't much in the bedroom except for the bed, a chair, and a chest of drawers.

The old man must be making pretty good money. He sold everything he caught, and nobody argued with him about the price. He had that thick bundle of money, all those fifty-dollar bills. And he was living no better than LeRoy's mother in Chicago.

If he didn't need the money, why did he work so hard? And since he had money, why didn't he spend it? It didn't make a whole lot of sense. Except for what the old man had said about not having the heart to build a house for strangers.

LeRoy went back outside and returned to work, cutting eight-foot-long two-by-fours out of the longer pieces of lumber in the stack. It wasn't hard, but it required concentration, and time went by quickly.

He was surprised when he heard a noise and looked up to see the old man coming out of the truck with his arms full. In one hand he held a bag full of groceries, and in the other, two bottles of wine.

"Still got all your fingers?" he asked. He was clearly in a good mood.

"Five on each hand," LeRoy said.

"Good, then you'll be able to eat a two-inch steak without any help."

"I thought you said steak wasn't for carpenter's helpers."

"It's not," the old man said. "But this is an occasion."

"What occasion?"

"Our horse came in. I had five dollars on his nose."

"You been betting on the horses?" LeRoy asked. He didn't believe it. "What about that sin and wickedness you're always talking about?"

"I'm sixty years old," the old man said. "And I work hard for my money, and I don't owe no man a dime that I can't pay. I can't see a thing wrong with me putting five dollars on a horse every once in a while." That little speech came out very strong, and for a moment LeRoy thought he'd provoked the old man. But then the old man's eyes lit up and he smiled. "The horse was named Instant Expert," he said. "I just couldn't let that go by without putting a little bet on him."

LeRoy laughed.

"Paid thirty-to-one," the old man said. "I figured that called for a steak." He reached in the bag and came out with an enormous steak, wrapped in transparent plastic. "What do you think of that?"

"I think you should have bet ten dollars," LeRoy said.

"Don't be greedy," the old man said. He looked around. "You clean up this mess and get those two-by-fours back under the tarp, and I'll start fixing supper."

As LeRoy cleaned up, he saw that the old man walked nearly to the water's edge with a bag of charcoal. He poured about half the charcoal right on the sand, sprayed it with charcoal lighting fluid from a can, and lit it. Then he went back into the shack.

When LeRoy had finished cleaning up, he carried the power saw, the extension cord, and the other stuff into the shack. The old man had peeled and cut potatoes, and he was wrapping ears of corn in aluminum foil. A pot of fat was heating on the stove.

"Open one of those wine bottles," the old man said. "And we'll have a little glass to give us an appetite."

"You're really feeling pretty good, aren't you?" LeRoy asked.

"Yeah, I'm feeling pretty good," the old man answered. "I thought about that on the way home. Now I got something to look forward to when the shrimping's over."

"I don't understand you," LeRoy said.

"Well, what I've been doing when the shrimping's

72

done is just tend the crab traps. That gets pretty dull, and there's not a whole lot of money in it."

"I don't understand what you mean about when the shrimping's done," LeRoy said.

"Well, they move out into the Gulf," the old man told him. "And that old boat and me, we're too old to do much Gulf shrimping."

"You mean, the shrimp aren't always out there?"

"That's right," the old man said. "Shrimp is a crop like any other. Some parts of the year, they're just growing. And some parts of the year, you can harvest them. We're just about finished with the harvest. You'll have to start thinking about getting yourself another job."

LeRoy became very uncomfortable when he heard that.

"What I'm going to do when the shrimping's done," the old man said, "is finish up the house. Give me something to do besides watch the waves go up and down." He had finished wrapping the corn in aluminum foil.

"How are you going to cook that steak?" LeRoy asked. He was really more interested in changing the subject than anything else. The idea of going to look for a job down here really bothered him.

"How did you think I was going to cook it?" the old man replied. LeRoy realized he had asked what the old man thought was another dumb question.

"I didn't see a stove out there," LeRoy said.

"No, you didn't," the old man said, and he smiled again. LeRoy recognized the smile. It meant the old man was about to show LeRoy something he had never seen or heard about before.

"So how are you going to cook the steak?"

73

"The oldest way, and some say still the best way there is," the old man said, smiling so that all his teeth showed. "I'm going to throw the meat in that fire, that's how I'm going to cook it."

"You're putting me on," LeRoy said.

"Well, while you're frying those potatoes," the old man said, "you just look out the window and see if I'm fooling or not." He raised his wine glass to LeRoy. "*Santé*," he said.

"*Santé* yourself," LeRoy said. The old man was up to something smart, even if LeRoy couldn't figure out what it was. He decided the old man probably had some sort of grill he would stick into the sand over the charcoal.

The old man searched around in the drawer with the knives and forks and came out with a thermometer. It was a regular, professional candy thermometer. LeRoy had seen them before in the Del Monte Cafeteria. It was the last thing in the world he expected the old man to have.

"Louis gave me that a couple of years ago," the old man said. "You have to get the fat 375 degrees, no more and no less, before you put the potatoes in."

"I've seen one before," LeRoy said.

"In your *cafeteria*, I expect?" the old man said. He didn't give LeRoy a chance to reply. "The fat's almost hot enough. When it gets to 375, you put the potatoes in." He laid the ears of corn on top of the steak and walked out of the kitchen with the plate and a pair of tongs.

LeRoy dipped the thermometer into the fat, waited until the fat was exactly 375 degrees, then

74

carefully slipped the potatoes into it. As soon as they were in, he went to the window.

The old man had put the aluminum-wrapped corn right on the charcoal. LeRoy had never seen that done before. He told himself that maybe there was something he didn't know, maybe the aluminum somehow kept the corn from burning. But there was no way, he told himself, no way at all, that you could just throw a piece of raw meat right onto charcoal without ruining it.

With one eye on the French-fried potatoes, he watched as the old man turned the corn with the tongs. What he's probably doing, LeRoy thought, is putting on a little show for me, to keep me guessing until the last second. Then he'll put some kind of grill over that fire, or maybe bring the steak back in here and cook it on the stove.

Finally, the old man took the ears of corn off the charcoal and sort of stacked them around the edges of the fire. He picked up the steak with the tongs, swung it back and forth, and then gently laid it right on top of the coals.

"Oh, no!" LeRoy groaned. The old man had gone and ruined a beautiful steak. There was a cloud of smoke from the charcoal, and now and then flames jumped.

A perfectly good steak, ruined. Ten dollars, at least, maybe more, just destroyed!

LeRoy didn't even want to look at it. He went to the stove and stirred the French-fried potatoes. They were cooking quickly. He would have to watch them, so they wouldn't be burned the way the steak had been.

He was taking the potatoes from the fat with a set of tongs, when the old man came back into the kitchen. LeRoy looked at the steak and confirmed what he had suspected. That beautiful piece of meat was charred black.

He saw the old man carefully spread butter on it and then shake something from a jar onto it.

"What's that?" he asked.

"Garlic powder," the old man answered. "Garlic *powder*, not salt."

"Think that'll take away the burned taste?" LeRoy asked.

"Well, I'll say this for you, boy, you just don't give up, do you? If you don't like this steak, you don't have to eat it. I like it about as well cold as I do fresh from the fire, so you don't have to worry about anything being wasted."

The old man took a large knife from a cabinet drawer and ran it up and down a sharpening steel with a practiced motion. He did it just as well, LeRoy admitted to himself, as any of the chefs in the Del Monte Cafeteria. Then the old man began to slice the steak into thin strips, about a quarter of an inch thick.

He cut three strips for himself, and three more for LeRoy. Then, using the knife like a shovel, he laid them on plates.

The inside of the steak, LeRoy saw, wasn't burned at all. It was pink.

"Now, you don't have to eat any of that," the old man said. "But I thought maybe you'd want to try just a mouthful."

LeRoy brought the potatoes to the table and sat down. "It don't smell bad," he said.

76

The old man put a piece of steak in his mouth. "Don't taste half bad, either," he said.

LeRoy cut a piece of the steak and put it in his mouth. He didn't understand why, but there was no burned taste at all. It was just perfect steak. The old man looked at him.

"It's all right, I guess," LeRoy said.

"That the best you can do, boy?" the old man said.

"Okay," LeRoy said. "I was wrong. It's delicious."

CHAPTER
8

Over the next couple of days LeRoy noticed that when they pulled the net, they hauled less shrimp than they had at first. There were still a lot of crabs, but crabs didn't bring in nearly as much money as shrimp. There were also more trash fish, mostly saltwater catfish, but also thousands of fish about the size of his thumb.

What the old man has said, that the shrimp were about to go out into the Gulf, was apparently true. That meant the old man's other observation was also true: It was almost time for LeRoy to find another job.

LeRoy didn't like the thought of that at all. He knew it wasn't because he didn't like to work, but because he would most likely end up in a kitchen someplace. And that meant he would have to start at the bottom all over again. He would be king of the pot washers, or chief floor mopper.

And there was nothing he could do about it. The old man had said both he and the boat were too old to go out into the Gulf. There was no arguing about that. LeRoy would just have to get a job. And that was that.

The following Monday, they didn't go out at all. The old man had decided it was time for LeRoy to take the driver's license examination. He sat at the breakfast table with the handbook from the state police, and asked LeRoy how far you had to park from a fire hydrant, what the speed limit was in towns and cities, and other questions he would have to be able to answer.

At nine o'clock, they drove into Pass Christian. A state trooper had set up shop in the waiting room of the Pass Christian police department. There were a dozen people trying to get driver's licenses. First the trooper checked their eyesight with an eye chart. Then he gave them all the written examination. LeRoy missed two of the twenty questions, but that gave him a score of 90 percent, more than he needed to pass. Finally, the trooper administered the road test. LeRoy was surprised at how easy that was. All he had to do was drive through town for a dozen blocks, turn the truck around, and finally park it.

They gave him his driver's license right on the spot. LeRoy had thought it would probably come in the mail in a week to ten days, but an hour and a half after he had gotten to the police station, he had a license, sealed in plastic, with his photograph on it. The photograph, he thought, made him look like a criminal on a wanted poster. But the address that appeared on the license made him feel like an official resident of Mississippi. LeRoy Chambers, it said, Rural Route One, Pass Christian.

LeRoy and the old man stopped at Jesse Hamm's lumberyard on the way back and picked up another load of supplies for the house. The old man said nothing about his getting a license. He didn't congratulate him.

Later, while LeRoy helped the old man nail studs together, he wondered about that. Finally, he decided the old man hadn't congratulated him on getting a driver's license because the old man just didn't think it was a big deal.

LeRoy didn't have much time to think. He was kept hopping. He knew exactly what he was doing with his hammer and power saw. One by one, he hammered the rough walls together, pushed them upright, and then maneuvered them into place over bolts the old man had set in the concrete slab with a tool that looked like a gun. It just shot the bolts into the concrete as if they were bullets.

By three o'clock, rough walls were up all around the outside of the slab.

"That's enough," the old man said. "We didn't have our lunch, and we've already done what four ten-dollar-an-hour carpenters would have done in two days." He looked at LeRoy and smiled. "You want something done right, boy, do it yourself," he said, waving his hand at the walls. That was a lot of work for two men to have done in a couple of hours, LeRoy thought. The old man was really something.

"Now what?" LeRoy asked.

"I've been wondering," the old man said, pushing him gently toward the shack on the edge of the concrete slab, "if you could go into New Orleans every day without getting lost or going to jail."

"What's that supposed to mean?" LeRoy asked. He didn't like that crack about going to jail. And now that he thought about it, he didn't like the crack about getting lost, either.

They went to the sink in the kitchen and washed their hands.

"You do any thinking about what those people in New Orleans we been selling shrimp to did today, when I didn't show up with any to sell them?" the old man asked.

"Yeah, I did, I guess."

"One of two things," the old man went on. "Either they didn't have any really fresh shrimp and crabs, or they bought them someplace else for a lot more money."

"So?" LeRoy asked.

"So I'm thinking about going back into the shrimp and crab business," the old man said. "Maybe some fish, and probably some crawfish, too, when they come into season."

"I don't understand."

"I did that years ago, when your grandmomma was alive, and before your daddy got sucked in by the big-city lights," the old man said.

"Did what?"

"Bought shrimp and crabs from other people, carried them to New Orleans, and sold it," he explained. "You don't get rich, but it's better than working for somebody else."

He looked at LeRoy as if he expected LeRoy to say something.

"Well?" the old man asked, finally.

"Well, what?"

"Think we ought to go into business? I'll buy the stuff, and you take it to New Orleans and sell it."

"Where are you going to buy it?"

"Right out there," the old man said, and pointed to the dock. "I'll get on the CB and spread the word that Aaron Chambers is back in business."

The old man was obviously happy with the idea.

"I thought everybody but you was selling their stuff to the fish market," LeRoy said. "Why would they switch to you?"

"Because when they come off the water, they can stop here first," the old man said. "Where I'll give them more for good stuff than they can get at the fish market."

"The fish market's not going to like that," LeRoy said.

"That's what they call the free enterprise system," said the old man.

"You really think we could do it?"

"There's one way to find out. That is, if you think we ought to do it."

"Yeah!" LeRoy grinned. "I think that's a fine idea!"

The old man walked to the truck, got in on the passenger's side, and took the CB microphone from the glove compartment. "If they haven't had a lot better luck than we had on Saturday," he said, "there's bound to be somebody still out there, trying to fill the ice chests." Then he spoke into the microphone. "Anybody still dragging on the sound?" he called. "Come back to Aaron Chambers."

The CB hissed and crackled for twenty seconds, and then a voice came on the air.

"This is the *Bonny Belle*, Mr. Aaron," the voice said. "You got troubles? I'm about five miles off Pass Christian Point. Come back."

"No troubles, *Bonny Belle*," the old man replied. "What I'm looking to do is buy two, three boxes of shrimp for cash money. Come back."

"I got a couple of boxes I guess I can let you have, Mr. Aaron. When do you want them? Come back."

"Anytime you can get them here. I'm not going anywhere. Come back."

"I'll be in there in an hour or so, Mr. Aaron. This is the *Bonny Belle*, clear."

The old man put the microphone back in the glove compartment and turned off the CB.

"He'll be in here just as soon as he can get his net out of the water," he said. There was a look of triumph on his face. "Cash money talks."

"Well, doesn't the fish market pay them?"

"Fish market takes an hour to make up a check, and then they have to worry about getting the check cashed," the old man said. "I'm going to put cash money in his hand."

"It looks like we're in business," LeRoy said.

"I'll go into New Orleans with you tonight," the old man said.

"Tonight?"

"Tonight. And you pay attention to where you're going because tomorrow you're going by yourself.

Now you start chipping ice for the coolers, and I'll get on the telephone and tell our customers we're coming."

Thirty minutes later, as LeRoy was chipping ice from the freezers on the boat, he heard the chug-chug-chug of a diesel engine. Looking up, he saw a shrimper easing up to the dock. He thought it would be the *Bonny Belle*, but the name *Gulf Princess* was lettered on her bow.

A crewman jumped off the bow and made a line fast. "We heard Mr. Aaron was buying shrimp," he said to LeRoy.

Just then, the old man walked onto the pier. "I'll take two boxes," he said. "Fourteen-to-eighteens, and I'll pay you a dime more a pound than the fish market."

Fourteen-to-eighteens were large shrimp. A pound would contain from fourteen to eighteen shrimp. A box of shrimp weighed a hundred pounds. The old man was offering the crewman twenty dollars more than he could get at the fish market.

"They're not sorted," the man said.

"LeRoy'll sort them," the old man said. "I just put on a pot of coffee. You fellas want a cup?"

"I'll call the others, Mr. Aaron," the crewman replied.

LeRoy watched the old man and the men from the shrimper walk up to the shack on the slab. Then he went through the piles of shrimp, picking out the fourteen-to-eighteens and throwing them onto a box on a scale.

LeRoy realized this wasn't going to be what he'd expected. He would be doing the work, sorting the shrimp, weighing them, icing them down, and finally delivering them to New Orleans. The old man would be sitting around here, drinking coffee. Some partnership!

But then he considered the alternative. He knew he would much rather be doing this than starting at the bottom again in some kitchen.

The *Bonny Belle* chugged up to the pier before LeRoy had finished sorting and icing the shrimp from the *Gulf Princess*.

"I heard Mr. Aaron was buying shrimp," the captain of the *Bonny Belle* shouted.

"We're paying a dime more a pound for fourteen-to-eighteens than the fish market," LeRoy told him.

"*We're* paying?" the captain asked. "Just who are you, boy?"

"I'm Mr. Aaron's grandson," LeRoy said.

"Well, I'll be," the man said. "I didn't know he had one." He turned and unloaded two boxes of shrimp from the deck of the *Bonny Belle*. "Sorted them on the way in," he said. "I sort of thought he'd want only the big ones." He looked at LeRoy. "You want to check them?" he asked.

"No, I'll trust you."

The man laughed. "Mr. Aaron wouldn't trust me," he said. "Where is he?"

"Up at the shack," LeRoy said.

"You better check those close," the man said, and walked down the pier and up to the shack. When LeRoy looked in the shrimp boxes, he found shrimp that were, if anything, larger than the fourteen-to-eighteens.

By the time he had finished packing the four

boxes — 400 pounds of shrimp — into smaller coolers and icing them down, he had used up just about all the ice in the freezers. He refilled the ice cartons, put them back in the freezer, and then loaded the iced-down shrimp onto the pickup truck.

Just as soon as he started toward the shack, the old man came out. LeRoy suspected that the old man had been watching from the window to see when he would finish.

The old man climbed into the passenger seat and handed LeRoy a map of New Orleans. He'd marked with a felt-tip pen the stops they were to make, and the route to follow. LeRoy counted the Xs, each indicating a stop. There were twenty-three of them.

"You called all these places?" LeRoy asked.

"I called six or seven," the old man said. "We'll just stop by the others and see if they want any."

"And if they don't? What if they already have their shrimp?"

"Then I guess we'll lose money," the old man said. "Come on, boy. Put this thing in gear and let's get going."

As they were crossing Lake Pontchartrain on the interstate bridge, the old man said, "We paid $2.25 a pound. That means we're going to have to get $2.60 a pound. That'll give us $140 for wear and tear on the truck, for the ice, and for our time."

"That's if we can sell all of it," LeRoy said.

"We'll just stay until we do. Worse comes to worst, we'll sell what's left over out of the back of the truck."

Worse didn't come to worst. By half-past nine they'd sold the last of the shrimp, and were on their way home. As soon as they got back on the interstate, the old man curled up against the door of the truck and went to sleep. Slavery wasn't dead, LeRoy thought. It was alive and well in Pass Christian, Mississippi. He had gotten up at half-past six, and except for breaks to eat, he'd been working ever since. Half-past six in the morning to half-past eleven at night was a seventeen-hour day, and the old man hadn't offered him a cent for the work he'd been doing.

The next day wasn't quite so bad. They got up with the birds, of course, and as soon as they had finished breakfast, went to work. LeRoy washed the dishes, while the old man worked on the house, nailing together roof trusses.

The first shrimp boat chugged up to the dock with one box of shrimp at noon. By half-past one, LeRoy had iced down another four hundred pounds of shrimp and packed them in the coolers. Then he went to New Orleans by himself. The restaurants expected him, and he cleaned out the truck by seven-thirty. When he got back to the shack, it was a little after nine. There wasn't a light. The old man had gone to bed.

Things were improving, LeRoy thought. He was down to a fifteen-hour day. He climbed into his bunk on the boat and fell fast asleep.

And the third day wasn't as bad as the second. It was dark when LeRoy got back from New Orleans, and there were no lights in the shack, but it was only eight o'clock. LeRoy stopped the truck and looked at the building in the light from the headlights. There were half a dozen roof trusses in place. How the old man had got them up there by himself was something LeRoy couldn't figure out. No wonder he went to bed at eight o'clock. He was worn out.

LeRoy went to the cabin on the boat and lay down, fully expecting to pass out immediately, as he had the previous two nights. But after ten minutes of tossing and turning, he realized that he wasn't all that tired. He certainly wasn't sleepy. He got out of bed and walked out front to the bow. He sat down on the rail and hung his feet over the side. Looking out over the water at the faraway lights and at the line of red channel markers, he thought: Boy, am I a long way from Chicago!

He wondered if this was what was going to happen to the rest of his life. Was he going to spend it all hauling shrimp to the back doors of restaurants?

Suddenly a bright glow of headlights on the road behind him startled LeRoy. He was even more surprised when the lights came down to the dock instead of going to the house. He swung his feet back onto the deck and then headed to the pier.

Whatever fool was driving the car, or the truck, or whatever it was, didn't have the manners to turn off the headlights. LeRoy was blinded by them.

"Who is that?" LeRoy shouted, shielding his eyes.

"Who did you expect this time of night?" the old man replied.

"Whose car is that?" LeRoy asked, walking down the pier. The old man saw him shielding his eyes and turned off the lights. LeRoy watched the headlights fade into little red dots. Then he could see hardly anything at all.

"What do you think?" the old man asked.

"What do I think about what?"

"About this thing," the old man said, thumping the fender with his fist. LeRoy's eyes were growing accustomed to the light. He saw that it wasn't a car, or a pickup, either. It was — he searched for the word — a carryall, a panel truck with windows and seats in the back. He wondered what the old man was doing with it.

"Where'd you get this?" LeRoy asked.

"Where do you think I got it? There's a place on the highway, with a big sign that says General Motors Trucks. They sell them there."

"You *bought* it?" LeRoy asked.

"Well, they sure didn't give it to me," the old man replied. "I hate to think how much I paid for it."

He pulled open the door. The interior lights came on. LeRoy walked closer to get a better look. There was enough light for him to see the door. It bore a painted sign:

A. CHAMBERS
&
Grandson
FRESH SHRIMP & CRABS
Pass Christian, Miss.

"I figured maybe you'd want to try it out," the old man said.

LeRoy didn't say a word. He climbed behind the wheel and pretended to be looking over the inside of the shiny new carryall. The truth of the matter was, he couldn't see well. His eyes were filled with tears.

"I expect," the old man said, "that if you washed

this thing out regular, you could keep the smell out of it. In case you wanted to take a girl to the movies or something." Then he reached over and very gently touched LeRoy's shoulder. "Good night, LeRoy," he said, and walked up to the shack.

CHAPTER
9

The only trouble LeRoy had with the carryall was keeping it under the speed limit. It just seemed to want to go a lot faster than the law allowed. Aside from that, it was great.

It was even air-conditioned. The old man had said he didn't "hold with air conditioning," and the only reason the carryall had it was that the dealer didn't have one in stock without it. But LeRoy noticed that the old man didn't complain any, or open the windows, when he got into the truck.

The two seats in the back had come out the very first morning. With the seats out, the carryall could carry more than the pickup truck had been able to, and getting the coolers in and out was a good deal easier. The extra space meant room for a dozen plastic buckets full of crabs, in addition to the shrimp.

The old man said they wouldn't give him half what the truck was worth, so he kept it. That meant there would always be something for LeRoy to drive. He hadn't met any girls (or anyone else, for that matter), but now that he had wheels, the situation was going to change. The only problem was the work-week — six days from six-thirty until seven-thirty or eight o'clock. It didn't leave a whole lot of time for socializing.

Not that that seemed so important. What really mattered now was "servicing the route," as the old man put it. For the first time, LeRoy was anxious to get on with his work.

And the carryall was responsible for another change, too, this one in LeRoy's appearance. One noontime, as he was getting into the carryall, the old man walked up to him, took the thick wad of bills from his trousers pocket, and peeled off two twenty-dollar bills. "There's an army-navy store on Chef Mentur Highway," the old man said. "Stop in before you service the route and buy yourself some khaki work clothes."

The old man didn't say it, but LeRoy knew what he was thinking. He didn't like LeRoy's choice of clothes. What had looked good, even great, in Chicago wasn't what you wore in Mississippi.

On the way to New Orleans, LeRoy thought about it. He didn't like khaki clothes, but he sure wasn't doing his threads any good wearing them to haul coolers of shrimp around. He decided to go along with the old man, and drove to the army-navy store on Chef Mentur Highway.

The clerk was a big, fat black man who asked, "You want them plain or embroidered?"

"Embroidered?"

The fat man wordlessly pulled a sample shirt from

92

beneath the counter. The shirt had "Pontchartrain Florists" embroidered on the back, and there was a smaller patch over the breast pocket that said "William."

"It's $4.95 for the back, and a buck for the front," the fat man said.

Thirty minutes later, LeRoy walked out of the place in khakis. The back of his shirt said "A. Chambers & Grandson," and over the breast pocket it said "LeRoy Chambers." He would come back in two days. By then, they would have three more shirts embroidered for him.

LeRoy thought he looked pretty nice, and decided it was just fine that people would now know he wasn't some kid hired to drive the carryall. On the way home, however, he wondered what the old man was going to say about it. The embroidering had cost almost as much as the shirt.

The old man looked at him kind of funny, but he didn't say anything.

"I had to take some money from the cash," LeRoy said. "I ordered three more shirts, and they made me pay in advance."

All the old man said was, "Make sure you get a receipt when you go back. That's a business expense, and we can take it off the income tax." But at breakfast the following morning, after he'd had time to think it over, he had another comment.

"I was thinking," he said, "that you ought to have something else stitched on your shirts."

"What's that?" LeRoy asked, falling right into the trap.

"Sew 'left' and 'right' on the cuffs," the old man said. "Then you wouldn't have to waste all that time in the morning trying to remember which arm goes where."

The old man's eyes lit up with delight, waiting for LeRoy's response.

"I was thinking of having 'other end up' stitched on the tail," LeRoy said. "But I didn't want to spend the money."

The old man laughed. "Those shirts look just fine, LeRoy," he said. "That was a good idea. If you look like you don't need the money, people don't argue with you about it. That's another reason I bought that new truck." Then he left LeRoy to do the breakfast dishes.

As he was washing the dishes, LeRoy noticed that there was a fresh stack of something under the plastic tarpaulin. When the old man pulled off the tarp, he saw it was a stack of plywood sheets. That was for the roof, obviously. Now LeRoy was curious to see how the old man was going to get them up there by himself.

Holding it over his head and sliding it up the roof truss, the old man got the first one up all right. But when he tried to put another sheet of plywood up the same way, the first one slid off. LeRoy started outside to help him, then stopped. Let him ask for help, he decided.

The old man tried for fifteen minutes before he came into the kitchen. "You want to give me a hand, boy?" he asked.

"You mean there's really something you can't do yourself?" LeRoy quipped.

"I'm perfect most of the time," replied the old man. "This is the exception that proves the rule."

Working together, they got the plywood onto the

roof trusses by nailing two sheets temporarily in place, then holding the others on top of them with half-driven nails.

As soon as all the wood was on the roof, LeRoy went down to the pier to take ice from the freezers. By the time he had loaded the day's shrimp and crabs, the old man had gotten almost all the plywood into place. When LeRoy went to the slab to say he was going, he found a big change in the way it looked. For the first time, LeRoy realized it was really going to be a house.

The old man saw him and climbed down the ladder.

"Well?"

"I was just thinking, it's starting to look like a house," LeRoy said.

"Yeah," the old man said. "I guess it is." He reached into his pocket for the roll of money.

"Some people," he said, "when they get a roof up, nail a little pine tree on top. They call it 'topping off.' Other people have a little drink to celebrate. That makes more sense to me. When you go by Le Cruet, tell Joe Keller I'd be obliged if he would sell me a good bottle of champagne."

Le Cruet was an expensive restaurant in the French Quarter.

"Champagne?" LeRoy asked.

"I don't build that many houses," the old man said. "And when I do, I like to do things right."

Joe Keller was a large, bald man with a thick German accent. But the old man had warned LeRoy never to call him a German. He was an Austrian, and Austrians did not like to be mistaken for Germans, even though they spoke the same language.

LeRoy had never seen him dressed in anything but spotless chef's whites.

"Aaron vants a nize boddle vine?" Joe Keller said. "My pleasure."

He led LeRoy into a large, cool room behind a heavy, locked door. LeRoy had never seen so much wine in one place before. There were thousands of bottles. Joe Keller went to the far corner of the room, picked up several bottles of wine, looked at them, put them back, and finally, after blowing the dust off one, handed it to LeRoy.

"Tell him he should drink it in goot healdt," Joe Keller said. LeRoy handed him a twenty-dollar bill. Joe Keller shook his head. "A liddle prezent between friends," he said. "My pleasure."

"He gave me the money to pay for it," LeRoy said. "I better pay for it."

Joe Keller wrinkled his mouth. "Your grandfadder's gooda hard head," he said. He snatched the twenty-dollar bill from LeRoy's hand. "Vait a second," he said, and went back to the wine rack. "Vun he pays for, vun is a liddle prezent." He handed LeRoy a second bottle of wine. "Dot's a nize liddle boddle vine."

"Mr. Keller," LeRoy said, "the old man said champagne."

"You shouldn't call your grandfadder 'old man,'" he said. "Shows no respect."

"He said *champagne*," LeRoy repeated. "You keep saying wine."

"Dot's champagne," Joe Keller said. "Champagne is vine vid bubbles from a place called Champagne, you understand? Vat's he vant it for, anyvay?"

"He just got the roof up on the house," LeRoy said. "He wants to celebrate."

"In dot caze," Joe Keller said, tucking the twenty-dollar bill in LeRoy's shirt pocket, "it's godda be a prezent."

"I better pay for it," LeRoy protested.

"I ain't going to *zell* you any," Joe Keller said. "How aboudt dot?"

There was nothing LeRoy could do but walk out of the kitchen of Le Cruet with a bottle of champagne in each hand. He put them in one of the coolers and finished working the route.

When he got back to Pass Christian, he found the old man sitting on the slab in one of the seats he'd taken out of the carryall. He was smoking a cigar. There was tarpaper board nailed to the walls, and the roof was completely covered.

LeRoy got the champagne bottles from the cooler and carried them onto the slab.

"This is the last time I'll have a chance to sit out in the open here," the old man said. "I'll have the rest of the walls covered tomorrow." He saw the two bottles. "I told you one bottle," he said.

"They're a present, both of them," LeRoy said. "He wouldn't take any money."

"Huh," the old man snorted. "Well, we'll put one of them away for the next celebration, and the next time I make some gumbo, I'll send him a pot."

LeRoy realized the old man was serious. He was going to send his cooking to the executive chef of a very fancy restaurant, and he seemed perfectly sure the chef would be glad to get it.

"There are a couple of champagne glasses under

the sink, wrapped in a towel," the old man said. "You get them."

The glasses were not only wrapped in a towel, they were tightly tied with string. It was obvious that they had been wrapped up a long time. There were three of them. LeRoy rinsed two under the tap, and then carefully dried them with a paper towel.

Then he carried them back onto the slab. The old man was opening the champagne. There was a sort of wire net around the neck of the bottle. The old man got it off, then sent the cork flying with a loud pop. He quickly poured champagne into the glasses.

"Be careful with those," he said. "Would you believe they're worth twenty-five dollars apiece? Least, that's what we were offered for them twenty years ago."

"You're putting me on."

"No, I'm not. They come down from your grand-momma's momma. We used to have eight of them. Hurricane got all but those three."

LeRoy sipped the champagne. He wasn't overly impressed.

"Good thing he didn't take your money," the old man said. "That wine's worth thirty dollars a bottle if it's worth a dime."

"Now you have to be kidding," LeRoy said. "It tastes like sour cider."

"That's because you don't know, that's all," the old man said. "Your ignorance is showing again."

"Thanks a lot," LeRoy said.

"You can't help it, of course," the old man said. "But that don't change things any. That's a really good bottle of wine. I'm wondering if it isn't too good for the priest."

"What priest?" LeRoy asked, now wholly confused.

"I was thinking that when we get the walls up, inside and out, and maybe lay some carpet, we'd get the priest, Father Dennis from Our Lady of the Sea, out here to bless it."

"Are you a Catholic?" LeRoy asked, surprised.

"No, but your grandmomma was. And I think she'd like it if I got the priest out here to bless the house. Can't see where it would hurt anything."

"If my grandmother was a Catholic," LeRoy asked, thinking out loud, "wasn't my father?"

"Yeah, he was, but I guess he didn't pay a whole lot of attention to what they tried to teach him," the old man said. And then he dropped the bomb. "Your mother called up a while ago, LeRoy," he said.

"She did? What did she want?"

"She said the cops had come to see her, looking for you. What she wanted to know was whether I thought she should tell them where you are."

"And what did you tell her?"

"I told her, sure, she should tell them."

"If they know where I am, they're liable to try to make me go back up there."

"Yeah, I expect that's why they were looking for you."

"Well, I'm not going," LeRoy said.

"You got to learn, boy," the old man said, "not to say things you can't back up."

LeRoy didn't say anything.

"I expect we'll have to give him some from the other bottle," the old man said. "Even if he won't appreciate it any more than you do. That's what your grandmomma would have done."

The old man was talking about the priest again. LeRoy wanted to keep arguing about whether he would have to go back to Chicago. But then he understood that as far as the old man was concerned, it was not something they could argue about. Well, there was nothing to discuss, anyway. He wasn't going to go, and that was it.

He took another sip of the champagne, draining the glass. He was surprised at himself when he reached for more. After he'd had the first couple of sips, he'd decided that he would drink one glass to please the old man, then quit. But the more he drank, the better it tasted.

The old man saw what he was doing.

"Grows on you, don't it?" he asked, and chuckled. "Every time I have a little champagne, I think it's a good thing I'm a poor man."

"Huh?"

"If I were rich, and didn't have to work," the old man said, "I could get to be a fat drunk in a hurry." That statement triggered another thought. "Where's the route money?" he asked.

LeRoy reached into his shirt pocket and handed it over.

The old man counted it. "If they keep catching shrimp," he said, "and you don't drive the truck into a wall, and people keep eating in restaurants, we just might make a go of this business." He handed LeRoy gas money, and wrapped the rest of the money around the wad he carried in his pocket.

"Those Wolves stick a knife in me," LeRoy said, "you're going to have to get you somebody else to service the route."

"Just because they got you thinking they're going to stick you with a knife don't mean it's going to happen."

"Now *your* ignorance is showing," LeRoy said, louder than he wanted to. "You don't know those guys. I do."

"We'll cross that bridge when we get to it," the old man said. "Hand me the bottle."

CHAPTER
10

Three days later, when LeRoy got back from New Orleans, early for once, he found a brown-and-white Ford parked nose-in to the slab. It had a decal with a six-pointed star on each door, and a chrome rack with a siren and a flashing blue light on the roof. On the front fender there was another decal, spelling out "Sheriff's Department" in reflective paint.

LeRoy's stomach hurt. He didn't know exactly what the sheriff's car meant, but he knew it wasn't good. He pulled up the carryall beside the patrol car and got out.

There was nobody in the kitchen of the shack when LeRoy walked in. But a moment later the old man and the sheriff came into the shack from what was now the inside of the house.

"You're back early," the old man said.

LeRoy looked between the old man and the sheriff.

"Mind your manners, boy. Say hello to Sheriff Greenhaw."

LeRoy saw that the sheriff's hand was wrapped around a can of beer. The old man had bought a case at the supermarket, to give to the shrimpers when they came in with their catch. LeRoy remained silent.

"How are you, boy?" the sheriff said. "I saw you in that new carryall, but I guess you didn't see me when I waved."

"No, I guess not," LeRoy said. He didn't remember seeing the sheriff at all.

"There's a couple of Yankee cops down at the office, LeRoy," the sheriff said. "They want to talk to you."

"I don't want to talk to them," LeRoy said.

"Sometimes," the sheriff said, finishing his beer and then absentmindedly crushing the can in his fist, "you have to do things you'd rather not do."

"I've got nothing to say to them," LeRoy said.

"They think it's pretty important," the sheriff said. "They came all the way down here from Chicago to see you. You're going to have to talk to them, boy."

LeRoy didn't reply.

"You want another beer, Ellwood?" the old man asked.

"Please, Mr. Aaron. And give LeRoy one, too," the sheriff said. "He looks all shook up."

The old man opened two cans of beer and handed one to LeRoy and one to the sheriff.

"I talked to them," the sheriff said. "And I talked to your grandfather about what happened up there," the sheriff said. "What you saw is important to them. And just giving them a statement isn't as bad as it could be."

"What could be worse?" LeRoy asked, and he realized it had come out sounding fresher than he really intended. Either the sheriff missed the freshness, or he chose to ignore it. He replied to the question.

"I don't know for sure what the law is in Illinois," he said. "But I don't expect it's much different from down here. Assault with a deadly weapon is a felony. In felony cases, when you have a witness who's not anxious to testify to what he saw, you can go to a judge and have him declared a material witness."

"What's that mean?"

"That means they can hold you, in jail if they want to, or at least on bond, to make sure you do testify."

"They're going to put me in jail?" LeRoy asked.

"You're not listening, boy," the old man said impatiently. "The sheriff said that's what they could do, if they wanted."

"What they told me, boy," the sheriff said, "was that all they wanted was a statement from you about what you saw happen. That's it. I asked them if they had a material-witness warrant, and they told me they didn't. If I was you, I'd give them the statement and get it over with."

"And if *I* was you," the old man said, "I'd do what the sheriff tells you, and thank him for his advice."

LeRoy gave the old man a dirty look. The old man was his grandfather; he was supposed to be on his side, not on the sheriff's.

"I'll be right there with you, boy," the sheriff said. "There's nothing to worry about. You didn't do anything wrong."

"When do I have to see them?" LeRoy asked.

"They're at the Sea View Motel," the sheriff said. "I told them I'd call them after I'd seen you. I figured you'd want your supper first."

"One of the boats brought me some nice bluefish, Ellwood," the old man said. "I was thinking I'd sauté them, and fry some potatoes. I'd be pleased if you'd eat with us."

"I'd be obliged to you, Mr. Aaron," the sheriff said. "It's been a long time since I had any of your bluefish. Not since Les moved away."

The old man didn't reply. He went to the refrigerator and took out the fish. Then he started to fillet it at the sink. Over his shoulder, he called to LeRoy to get some potatoes and peel them.

After eating, they rode to the courthouse in the sheriff's car. The old man sat up front with the sheriff. LeRoy rode in back. The sheriff's car was equipped with a metal shield that fitted across the top of the front seat. It was to protect the people in the front seat from those in the back. The shield was folded out of the way, but when he looked at the doors and saw that the inside handles had been removed, LeRoy felt like a prisoner.

LeRoy had presumed that the two cops from Chicago would be the skinny cop from the housing project and the junkie, the plainclothes narc named Moriarity. But Moriarity wasn't at the sheriff's office. The skinny cop was there with an older white man, tough-looking. There was also a woman with what

105

looked like a tiny typewriter, which sat on four wobbly-looking legs.

"How goes it, LeRoy?" the skinny cop asked, smiling and putting out his hand. He was wearing a blue business suit.

"What do you say?" LeRoy replied, and shook his hand.

"This is Sergeant MacMillan," the skinny cop said. The older cop shook LeRoy's hand as if he would have preferred not to. "And you must be Mr. Chambers," the skinny cop said to the old man. "My name is Paul Davis. I'm a Chicago housing authority police officer."

"Pleased to meet you," the old man said, shaking his hand.

"We can handle this, Sheriff," Sergeant Mac-Millan said. "No need for you to stick around. We appreciate your help."

"I'll stick around," Sheriff Greenhaw said, and settled himself in the chair behind his desk.

"What we're going to do, LeRoy," the skinny cop said, "is get your statement. This lady is a court reporter. That little machine she has is a stenotype machine. She can write down what's said just about as fast as you can talk, but try to talk slow enough and loud enough for her to hear you clearly. When she's finished, she'll type it all up, and then you can read it. When you're sure that she's typed exactly what you said, we'll ask you to sign it. And we'll ask the sheriff since he's here, to witness your signature. You understand all this?"

"I understand," LeRoy said.

"Okay, then, we'll get started," the skinny cop said.

106

Sergeant MacMillan pulled his chair close to Le-Roy's. He sat down, crossed his legs, and took out a notebook.

"This is an interview with Mr. LeRoy Chambers," he said, "conducted by Sergeant Richard MacMillan, Shield Number 405, Chicago Police Department, on April 19, in the office of the Sheriff, Gautier County, Mississippi. Present are Officer Paul Davis, of the Chicago housing authority police, and Sheriff Ellwood Greenhaw.

"First, Mr. Chambers," he said, "I want to advise you of your rights. You are not required to answer any questions which may tend to incriminate you, and you are entitled to be represented by legal counsel. Do you understand those rights?"

"Grandfather?" LeRoy asked. He was confused.

"Ellwood?" the old man asked, turning to the sheriff.

"LeRoy," Sheriff Greenhaw said, "I'll tell you not to answer any questions you shouldn't. Or we can get a lawyer for you, if you want one."

"The sheriff will watch out for you," the old man said. "Go on, answer their questions."

"And I wish to advise you, Mr. Chambers," the white cop went on, "that it is a criminal offense under the laws of Illinois to knowingly give false information to a police officer conducting a criminal investigation. Do you understand that?"

"Yeah, I understand it."

"Okay. For the record, you are LeRoy Stanley Chambers, formerly of 610 Hoover Housing Project, Chicago, Illinois, now temporarily residing at Rural Route One, Pass Christian, Mississippi. Is that right?"

"That's right."

"Were you residing at the Hoover Housing Project on March third of this year?"

"Yes."

"At approximately ten P.M. on the third of March, were you at the Hoover Housing Project, and, if so, what, if anything, did you see?"

There was a long pause. The white cop raised his eyebrows.

"Tell him what you saw, boy," the old man said. "Tell him just what you told me."

Everybody was looking at LeRoy: the skinny cop from the project, Sergeant MacMillan, Sheriff Greenhaw, the old man, even the lady with the stenotype machine. There was nothing to do but tell what had happened when he got off the elevator and found Elton, Howard, and B.J. working over old Mrs. Carson. So he told the story.

And the old man made it worse. "Why didn't you try to help her?" he asked.

LeRoy just looked at him.

"Mr. Chambers," the skinny cop intervened, "if LeRoy had tried to do anything, he'd probably have gotten badly hurt. These kids are real animals."

The look on the old man's face told LeRoy he thought both the skinny cop and LeRoy weren't really men. The skinny cop saw it, too.

"Most of the time, Mr. Chambers," he said, "the police patrol in pairs."

The old man didn't say anything, but it was clear that he still felt LeRoy should have done something.

Then Sergeant MacMillan asked him about what had happened after he'd talked to Officer Davis and the junkie. LeRoy told that story, too, including the part about getting his buttons cut off and his leather jacket slashed. Then he asked, "What difference does that make?"

"Well, I think we'll just hit those guys with an additional charge of assault with a deadly weapon," Sergeant MacMillan said.

"That won't stick, Sarge, and you know it," the skinny cop said. "Besides LeRoy, there were no witnesses."

"It'll give those punks something to read in the cell," Sergeant MacMillan said.

"I thought two of them were out on bail," LeRoy said.

"Not now they're not," MacMillan said. "They're in, charged with first-degree murder."

"What!"

"Mrs. Carson died, LeRoy," the skinny cop said. "That makes it murder."

"You didn't tell me that," Sheriff Greenhaw said. He sounded angry. Sergeant MacMillan shrugged his shoulders.

"If that woman is dead," the old man said, "then that makes LeRoy the only witness, doesn't it?"

Even as the unpleasant truth sank in, LeRoy wondered why he hadn't thought of it first.

"Yes, it does," Sergeant MacMillan said.

"You told me assault with a deadly weapon," Sheriff Greenhaw said. "That's all you said, A.D.W."

Sergeant MacMillan shrugged his shoulders again.

"Let me tell you my priorities, Sheriff," he said. "I've got an open murder-one case. An old lady knifed in a robbery. And I've got a witness. With that witness, I can put three animals away for a long time. Without that witness, all I've got is an unsolved murder. Now, this boy doesn't want to testify, and I'm sympathetic about that, I'm sorry for him. But either he testifies, or these three guys walk. You understand that, of course."

"You should have told me what you had," Sheriff Greenhaw said. "I'm entitled to that."

"Okay, I'm sorry," Sergeant MacMillan said. "But I had to put a bag on the kid, you can see that. With the statement, it'll be that much easier to get him declared a material witness."

"Which is what you were really after all the time, wasn't it?" Sheriff Greenhaw said.

"That's it. As a material witness, there's no place he can run."

"He could refuse to sign the statement," the sheriff said. "You think about that? Or he could go on the witness stand and lose his memory. You think about that?"

"If he signs the statement," MacMillan said, "it will be easier to get a material-witness warrant. But I can get one, anyway. I hope it doesn't come to it, but I'm prepared to serve a warrant on him. You heard what he said, after being advised of his rights. That's just about as good as a statement."

"My grandson," the old man said, "is going to sign your statement, Sergeant, and he will testify."

"Thank you," Sergeant MacMillan said. "Mr. Chambers, I promise you we'll see that nothing happens to him in Chicago. And there's no way they can get to him down here. They don't know where he is."

"Yes, they do," LeRoy said. "The first question you asked me was where I lived. They'll find out where I am."

"I don't think you need worry about them coming down here," Sergeant MacMillan said.

"Maybe they won't," LeRoy said. "But what about my mother? They already tore up her apartment."

"We'll protect your mother in Chicago," Sergeant MacMillan said. "And I'm sure Sheriff Greenhaw can keep things under control down here."

"They come down here," the old man said firmly, "they'll be sorry they did."

"I'm sure, as I said, Mr. Chambers," Sergeant MacMillan repeated, "that Sheriff Greenhaw will be able to handle the situation."

"I'm not talking about Sheriff Greenhaw," the old man said. "I'm talking about me. No offense, Ellwood."

Sheriff Greenhaw laughed. "None taken, Mr. Aaron," he said. "Maybe we're all making a mountain out of a molehill. But if you want to talk about tough and mean, Sergeant, I don't think your three punks ever came up against an angry Mississippi fisherman protecting his own."

"You better believe it," the old man said. LeRoy thought he was very proud of himself. He also thought he was a fool. He didn't know the Wolves, and neither did Sheriff Greenhaw.

"Miss Elly," Sheriff Greenhaw said, "I think you can go and type up that statement. LeRoy's going to sign it, aren't you, boy?"

It took an hour for the stenographer to type up a record of the interview. While she was typing it, the skinny cop explained to LeRoy and the old man what was going to happen next. The case would be brought before a grand jury. That wasn't the trial.

The grand jury just determined whether or not the police had enough of a case to bring Elton, Howard, and B.J. to trial. If they thought there was enough evidence — in other words, if they believed what LeRoy said, and there was no reason they wouldn't believe it — the grand jury would return an indictment. The trial would follow that.

"You mean, I'll have to testify twice?" LeRoy asked.

"I'm afraid so," the skinny cop said. "There won't be much to the grand jury, but when you get to trial, you might as well know that their defense lawyer is going to try to make you look like a fool and a liar."

"And what if I just don't show up?" LeRoy asked.

"Shut your fool mouth, LeRoy," the old man said.

"You'll be there, LeRoy," the skinny cop said, "if we have to come back down here and carry you up in handcuffs."

"There won't be any need for that," the old man said. "We'll be there."

And then the lady returned with the typed statement in four carbon copies, and LeRoy signed all of them. Then Sheriff Greenhaw signed, as a witness.

"You really going to go through with the material-witness warrant?" the sheriff asked. "If Mr. Aaron says LeRoy will be there, you can count on it."

"In my shoes, Sheriff, what would you do?" Sergeant MacMillan replied. Sheriff Greenhaw shrugged his shoulders.

In the patrol car on the way back to the house, Sheriff Greenhaw turned halfway around to speak to LeRoy.

"LeRoy, you understand that there's no way to

stop things now? I mean, I hope you're not thinking of running away, or anything like that. They'd find you, just as sure as night follows day."

"You didn't have to say that, Ellwood," the old man said.

"I didn't like saying it, Mr. Aaron," the sheriff said. "But I did have to say it."

"You just tell us where and when you want LeRoy, and we'll be there," the old man said. "It's as simple as that."

CHAPTER
11

That night the old man didn't say anything about what had happened, and he didn't bring up the subject the next morning, either. The shrimp boats started coming in about half-past nine, and by noon LeRoy had a truckload iced down and ready to go.

He thought about it driving into New Orleans. But once he got there, working the route didn't give him much time to think about anything at all.

On the way home, he started feeling sorry for himself. It didn't seem fair that he should have to have all this trouble with the Wolves just because he had gotten off the elevator at the time they were robbing Mrs. Carson. All he really wanted out of life, he thought, was what he had now. An interesting job, away from the project.

The old man still hadn't said anything about paying him, but, on the other hand, LeRoy hadn't actually asked for money. He didn't have anything to spend it on. Then he remembered the old man had made a remark about washing the back of the carryall in case he wanted to take somebody to the movies. Taking somebody to the movies meant he would need money, and the old man knew that.

There *was* money around. Every day LeRoy took home $120, $140. He was spending $15 every other day for gas, and a couple of dollars every day for something to eat when he was in New Orleans. But they were making maybe $50 a day, clear, maybe a little more. The carryall had cost a lot of money, but the old man hadn't said anything about buying it on time, which meant that he had had the cash for it. And he was putting a lot of money into supplies to build the house. LeRoy thought he probably had that, too, put away in a bank. All they had to pay for was food, electricity, and gas for the stove. They were making it.

Everything would be just fine, if it weren't for the cops and the Wolves. Why couldn't the cops leave him alone?

It was easy to get mad at the cops, but LeRoy had to admit they were just doing their job. He hauled shrimp, and the cops put people in jail. That left the Wolves to blame. But the Wolves were mad at him, and were liable to knife him or, worse than that, get at him through his mother. And despite what Sergeant MacMillan and the skinny cop had said, LeRoy didn't think there was anything they could do to stop them.

And what if he went ahead and testified, and the jury didn't believe him? What if the jury turned them loose? They weren't just going to walk out of the courthouse and forget the whole thing. They'd get back at him. Even if they went to jail, there would still be other Wolves on the loose.

The cops knew what the Wolves were capable of. They wouldn't be surprised to find him dead in an alley, with a dozen stab wounds in him. But what they were after was putting the guys who had killed Mrs. Carson behind bars, getting them off the streets. As far as they were concerned, it was a pretty good swap, one good guy for three bad guys. That made a lot of sense, if you didn't happen to be the good guy.

The old man didn't really know what it was like. Everything was black and white to him. The Wolves had killed Mrs. Carson, so they should get punished for it. And he thought the cops could handle the whole thing. He thought that once you did what the cops wanted you to do, that would be the end of it. He just didn't understand what it was like in the project. Doing what the cops wanted you to do was a good way to get yourself killed.

LeRoy wished it could be the other way, the way it was on television. That he could just go to court and point out the bad guys. The bad guys would go to jail, and the cops would shake his hand. Justice would be done.

But that's not the way it was. To the Wolves, *he* was the the bad guy. And justice, for them, would be sticking knives in him for squealing to the cops. That's the way they saw things.

He had two sets of people, the cops and the old man on one side, and the Wolves on the other, both telling him to do "right" or face the consequences.

116

And no matter what he did, one group wouldn't like it. He was right in the middle.

It would be easy to say, I will do what I know is right — if doing right didn't mean getting himself cut, or killed. Or having them get after his mother if they couldn't get at him.

When he got back to the house, the headlights picked out something shiny from a long way off. When he got closer, he saw that the old man had started to put windows in the walls. They were aluminum, and it was the metal strapping holding them together that had reflected the headlights.

The old man was in the kitchen. There was a bottle of wine on the table, and two small but thick steaks.

"I got you a bed," the old man said immediately.

"A bed?"

"I got the windows up in your room. And it was either go get you a bed, or put up some more windows. I figured I'd already done a fair day's work."

He walked out of the kitchen into the house. He snapped a switch, and lights came on. That surprised LeRoy, because he didn't remember any lights. He looked at it. It was only a socket and a bulb, hanging from the ceiling. But the old man had obviously put the wires in that day, too.

And LeRoy realized he couldn't see all the way across the slab to the walls anymore. The old man had half finished a room on the front, overlooking the bay. There was no door to the room, and the walls were just the insulation, stapled to the two-by-fours, but it was now a room. Another bare bulb hung down from the two-by-fours overhead. The room was still open to the rafters.

But there was a bed. The old man had even made it up, and the covers were turned down. And there was a chair beside the bed. Everything was new.

"I figured you were getting tired of sleeping on the boat," the old man said.

"Thank you," LeRoy said. He went and sat on the bed and smiled up at the old man. "Yeah," he repeated. "Thanks a lot."

"Your mother called again," the old man said. "I told her she ought to call later, when you were back from New Orleans."

"What did she have to say?" LeRoy asked.

"She got all shook up when I told her, yes, you drove in there all by yourself, and, no, I didn't think you were a little too young to be driving by yourself."

LeRoy smiled. "Is that all?" he asked.

"She said there was a story in the newspaper," the old man began. Then he interrupted himself. "Come on, let's go eat. I'm hungry."

LeRoy got off the bed and followed the old man out of his room.

"Turn the light off," the old man said. "Electricity costs a fortune these days."

LeRoy found the switch. He realized he had never seen a switch before, not the whole thing. It was a metal box, nailed to one of the two-by-fours. A heavy gray wire led down to it from where the ceiling would be. The wall, when the old man got that up, would fit flat with the front of the switch. The old man was really something; there didn't seem to be anything he couldn't do.

LeRoy turned the lights off and then on and then off again.

118

"You surprised to see it work?" the old man asked.

"I'm impressed," LeRoy said. "I thought you had to be an electrician to put lights in."

"You do," the old man said. He walked down what was going to be the corridor when the walls were all up, and into the kitchen. He took a corkscrew and opened the bottle of wine.

"The trouble with being in the fish business," he said, "is that after a while, you can't work up an appetite for the stuff. So I got us some steaks."

"You ought to make a deal with a butcher," LeRoy said. "You give him shrimp, and he gives us steaks."

"I used to do just that, before the supermarkets come," the old man said. "But the supermarkets want cash money, no swaps."

"What did my mother say about the newspapers?" LeRoy asked.

"Oh, yeah. There was a story that said the police have a witness to what those bums did to that old lady. She said they must be talking about you, and that we'd probably be hearing from the cops."

"Huh!" LeRoy snorted.

"So I told her they'd already come and gone," the old man said. "She said to give you her love."

"That all?"

"She said I was to tell you to drive careful," the old man said. He changed the subject. "I got butter beans and French-cut green beans. Which do you want?"

"I don't know what butter beans are," LeRoy said. The old man handed him a package of frozen beans.

"These are lima beans," LeRoy said.

"They're butter beans," the old man insisted.

"It says lima beans on the label," LeRoy said.

"I don't care what it says on the label," the old man said. "I know a butter bean when I see one."

"I'll have the lima beans," LeRoy said.

"*Butter beans* it is," the old man said, taking the package back from him. "I started the fire before. And the potatoes are cut and ready." He walked out of the kitchen carrying the steaks.

They ate on the pier, sitting on folding aluminum chairs, with the floodlight from the boat shining on them.

"I was going to wait until I had the house finished," the old man said, "and then build a porch. What I'm thinking now is that I'll get some lumber right away and build a porch, then finish the house. Won't take me but a day or two. Give us someplace to sit."

LeRoy didn't care when the old man built a porch, or even *if* he built one. He had other things on his mind.

"What could they do to me," he asked, "if I went to Chicago and said I really couldn't remember what had happened?"

The old man pretended he hadn't heard him.

"I could use concrete blocks," he said, "or I could set a row of six-by-sixes in concrete. Half a dozen one way, six the other."

"You heard me," LeRoy said.

"I could lay two-by-sixes a quarter of an inch apart," the old man went on. "What they call a deck, I think. That would probably be better than anything else."

"What if I said I couldn't remember anything?" LeRoy said loudly.

"Scared, are you?" the old man asked.

"Yeah, I'm scared. So what?" LeRoy said.

"Sometimes, when people are scared, they don't think too clearly," the old man said.

"I'm thinking clearly," LeRoy said. "And it's not just me I'm scared about. Those guys already tore up my mother's apartment. Knocked down a steel door with a fire extinguisher to get in. Don't tell me I'm not thinking clearly."

"The minute the cops arrested those boys," the old man said, "they were sure you told the cops what you had seen."

"I hadn't told the cops anything," LeRoy said.

"Facts don't count," the old man said. "What people believe is what counts. And they believe you told on them. And now that you've been declared a material witness, they know it for sure."

"But if I went up there and said I didn't see them working over Mrs. Carson, they would know I hadn't squealed on them."

"That's what I mean about scared people not thinking clearly," the old man said, taking a deep swallow of his wine.

"What's that supposed to mean?" LeRoy asked.

"Well, for one thing, you're not *squealing* on anybody," the old man said. "There's a big difference between telling the teacher that Tommy was the one who threw the blackboard eraser and swearing in court you saw three bums attack an old lady with a knife," the old man said. "And, even if you did get up in court and, after swearing on a Bible that you would tell the truth, lied about what you saw, it wouldn't do you any good with those bums. They'd just figure you changed your mind because you were scared. If you changed your mind once, you could change it again. You're going to have to stick with this thing to the end, boy, and that's all there is to it."

LeRoy wanted to argue with the old man. But he couldn't think of anything to say. The old man was right.

Five days later, while LeRoy was icing down a cooler full of shrimp, a sheriff's patrol car rolled up to the house. It wasn't Sheriff Greenhaw. It was a deputy LeRoy had never seen before.

LeRoy knew that the deputy was here for him, but he went on working as if the deputy were just paying a social call on the old man. After a couple of minutes, the deputy came out of the house, got back into his car, and drove off. Then the old man, still wearing his carpenter's apron, and with a flat-sided pencil stuck in his hair over his ear, walked down to the pier.

"Sheriff wants to see you," he announced.

"What about?"

"You know what about," the old man said. "You better get on down there."

"You're not coming with me?" LeRoy asked, without thinking, and was immediately embarrassed that he had.

"I figure you can find the courthouse without a map or me," the old man said. "I'll have the carryall loaded when you get back. You take the old truck."

"He didn't say what he wanted me for?" LeRoy persisted.

"All he did was send the deputy to get you," the old man said. "I told the deputy you'd come yourself. People saw you in a police car, they'd be liable to think you'd done something wrong."

LeRoy changed into the khaki shirt and trousers with "A. Chambers & Grandson" embroidered on the back before he drove into town. He would have changed, anyway, when he'd finished icing down the shrimp, and he didn't think he should go into town smelling like a shrimp boat.

He wished the old man had come with him. Then he was ashamed for thinking that. He wasn't a little boy who needed to hang on to somebody's hand. But when he walked into the courthouse and down the corridor to the frosted glass door of the sheriff's office, he realized that he really wished the old man were with him, no matter what it looked like.

A stout white woman sat behind a desk in the outer office. She looked up at him. She didn't say anything, but "Who are you and what do you want?" was written all over her face.

"I'm LeRoy Chambers," LeRoy said. "Sheriff Greenhaw sent for me."

"Have a seat," she said. "The sheriff's got somebody in with him."

LeRoy sat down on an old, plastic-covered couch and picked up a magazine. The sheriff kept him waiting about thirty minutes. Finally, the door to his office opened and a sergeant of the state troopers came out. The sheriff shook the sergeant's hand, and then, without smiling, waved to LeRoy, telling him to come in.

The sheriff walked behind his desk, sat down, and waved his hand again, this time signaling LeRoy to sit down in a chair in front of the desk. The plastic upholstery of the chair was still warm from the state trooper sergeant.

"LeRoy," the sheriff began, "you know what 'reciprocal extradition' means?"

"No, sir," LeRoy said.

"It's an agreement between two states, meaning that if the police in one state want somebody in the other state, they can have him. If somebody down here, for example, sticks up a store and then runs off to Illinois, the Illinois police will send him back here. And vice versa. You understand?"

"I understand."

"Well, we've got reciprocal extradition with Illinois," the sheriff said, and paused. "And what I have here," he continued, picking up several long sheets of stapled-together paper, "is a request from the State of Illinois about you."

LeRoy didn't say anything.

"It's from their attorney general to our attorney general," the sheriff went on. "He asks that the State of Mississippi take you into custody as a material witness in a murder case. And this sheet of paper is an order from our attorney general to me. It says" — and he started to read it — "that I am 'directed to locate and take into custody one LeRoy Chambers, presently believed to be residing in Pass Christian, and to deliver said LeRoy Chambers into the hands of the police department of Chicago, Illinois, when requested.' "

"You mean, I'm arrested?"

"Just about," the sheriff said. Then he read some more. " 'You will inform this office when the said LeRoy Chambers has been taken into custody. You will insure that the said LeRoy Chambers does not leave your jurisdiction, either by confining him in the county jail, or by causing him to post a cash or property bond in sufficient amount, which in your judgment will insure his availability to the Chicago Police Department when requested.' "

"I'm going to jail?" LeRoy asked.

"Let me finish," the sheriff said, somewhat impatiently. He picked up another sheet of paper. "This is going out with the morning's mail," he said. "It's a letter from me to the attorney general. It says that I have located you, taken you into custody, and informed you that you are a material witness and are to be turned over to the Chicago police when they ask for you. It also says that I have released you after you posted a sufficient cash bond."

"You mean the old man, my grandfather, is going to put up bail for me?" LeRoy asked.

"No, I mean *you're* going to put up bail," the sheriff said.

"I don't have any money."

"They didn't tell me how much of a bond," the sheriff said. "They just said a 'sufficient' bond. As far as I'm concerned, ten dollars is sufficient. If you don't have ten, I'll loan it to you."

"Ten dollars? That's all?" LeRoy asked, surprised.

"I'd consider it a favor if you didn't tell anybody how much," the sheriff said.

"Thank you very much," LeRoy said. It was the last thing LeRoy had expected.

"Don't get carried away," the sheriff said. "Let me tell you how I feel about this. First of all, I want you to understand that I'm on the side of the Chicago police. I didn't like the way that sergeant came in here and kept me in the dark, but that doesn't change anything. I understand why they want you, and I'm going to do whatever I have to do to turn you over to them. I want you to have that straight in your mind."

"Okay," LeRoy said.

"Now, I've got a couple of other options," the sheriff said. "The easiest thing for me to do would be call the turnkey in here and tell him to lock you up. I could even send the Chicago police a bill for your room and board. The other thing I could do would be get your grandfather in here to give me a property bond or a cash bond. In a murder case, a bond is usually five thousand dollars. That means Mr. Aaron would have to sign a paper saying he would put up either property worth five thousand dollars, or five thousand in cash money. Or he would have to go to a bondsman and pay him five hundred dollars, ten percent of the five thousand dollars. You understand all this?"

"Yeah, I understand."

"Say 'Yes, sir' to me, boy," the sheriff said. "I'm as old as your father."

"Yes, sir," LeRoy said.

"But I prefer to do what I've done," the sheriff said. "And I think you better know why. For one thing, I've known your grandfather and your father all of my life. I used to work on a shrimp boat with your father when we were younger than you are. I never knew him to lie. I don't know what the trouble is between him and your grandfather, and it's none of my business. As for your grandfather, I've known Mr. Aaron — and let me tell you, I don't like one little bit your calling him 'old man' — I've known

Mr. Aaron all of my life, and he doesn't say anything he doesn't mean. So what I'm doing is for your daddy and your grandfather, not for you. I don't know you. If Mr. Aaron says you'll do what you're supposed to do, I'll take his word. I'm not going to see him spending money on you, or putting up his property to keep you out of jail."

"I see," LeRoy said.

"And let me tell you this, too," Sheriff Greenhaw said. "If you should decide to break your word to me, and run, I'll find you, and I will put you in jail, and I guarantee you won't like it in there. You understand me, LeRoy?"

"Yes, sir," LeRoy said.

"You got any questions?" the sheriff asked.

"In that paper you read, it said I wasn't supposed to leave your jurisdiction," LeRoy said. "What about my going to New Orleans with the carryall?"

"You caught that, huh?" the sheriff said. "Well, I thought about that, too. You go ahead and do whatever you would normally do. Just be ready to come in when I send for you. Okay?"

"How am I going to get from here to Chicago?" LeRoy asked. "Are they going to send somebody after me?"

"Either that," the sheriff said, "or I'll have one of my deputies fly you up there. Probably that. Give somebody here a chance to fly to Chicago."

"Fly?"

"It's a long ride on a bus," the sheriff said.

"Yeah, I know," LeRoy said. "I came down here on a bus." He smiled. The sheriff smiled back at him.

"I didn't mean to talk nasty to you, LeRoy," he said. "But I wanted you to know how things are."

"Thank you," LeRoy said. He took out his wallet and handed Sheriff Greenhaw two five-dollar bills.

"Don't look so unhappy," the sheriff said. "You'll get them back."

CHAPTER
12

When he got back to the house, LeRoy found the carryall loaded and ready to go to New Orleans, as the old man had promised. But there was also a pile of shrimp headed and shelled and ready for the pan. "Big ones," the old man said. "I figured we might as well eat 'em, instead of some stranger from Phoenix, Arizona, or someplace, who wouldn't appreciate them."

The first thing LeRoy thought was that the old man had decided it would be cheaper for LeRoy to eat here than in New Orleans, but he quickly changed his mind. What the old man wanted was a chance to find out what had happened at the sheriff's office. He didn't come right out and ask, but that's what he was after; there was no question about it.

And as LeRoy told him, he understood that the old man hadn't really known what the sheriff was going to do when the material-witness warrant came down from Chicago. In other words, what had happened with the sheriff had not been set up between him and the old man. Did that mean the old man knew Sheriff Greenhaw would do what he could to make things easier for LeRoy? Or did it maybe mean that the old man thought LeRoy should stand on his own two feet, and face his problem by himself?

When LeRoy had told him what had happened, that he was out on a ten-dollar cash bond, the old man said, "Ellwood Greenhaw is a good man. But I'll tell you one thing: His bite is worse than his bark. I would hate to have him mad at me. Don't ever think that because he made this easier for you than he had to, he can be pushed around."

"What would you have done if he had put me in jail?" LeRoy asked.

"I'd have done what I could to get you out," the old man said. Then he smiled. "Sent you a cake with a hacksaw baked in, maybe."

"I just thought of something," LeRoy said. He didn't feel like smiling at all. "What happens in Chicago?"

"You know what happens in Chicago," the old man said.

"What I mean," LeRoy said, "is that the Chicago cops haven't known you all their life. They didn't work with my father on a shrimp boat when they were kids."

"What are you talking about?"

"I'm talking about when I get to Chicago, they're probably going to put me in jail, that's what I'm talking about," LeRoy said.

He could tell from the look on the old man's face

that he hadn't thought about that. Somewhat lamely, the old man said, "You don't know that for sure. And, anyway, they probably have some special place for material witnesses. You're not a criminal."

"They're going to put me in jail," LeRoy said. "You know they are."

"I think you better cross that bridge when you get to it," the old man said. "There's nothing you can do about it, anyway. There's no sense worrying about things you can't control."

"You don't know about jail in Chicago," LeRoy said.

"A jail is a jail," the old man said. "I know about jails."

LeRoy had a shrimp on his fork, ready to put in his mouth. Then he laid it down on the plate and stood up. He had lost his appetite. He walked out of the kitchen toward the carryall.

The old man followed him outside. As LeRoy got behind the wheel of the carryall, the old man called out to him, "Everything's going to be all right, boy. Don't let your imagination run away with you."

LeRoy didn't answer him. He started the engine, put the carryall in gear, and drove off.

He was running late, even though the old man had loaded the truck for him. The first three places he stopped on the route mentioned it, two of them nicely, saying they were afraid that maybe he wasn't going to show up, and the third not nicely. "You're late with this stuff," the chef told him. "You're screwing up our schedule."

There was nothing he could do but say he had been delayed, and that he would try to keep it from happening again.

And then he got to Alfred's Steak & Chop House. That was the first restaurant in New Orleans he'd ever been in, the one the old man had taken him to the night he'd gotten off the bus.

When he set the cooler with forty pounds of headed shrimp on the stainless-steel work table, one of the cooks walked over to him. He opened the lid, looked in casually, and said, "Alfred wants to see you, kid."

Alfred, *Mr.* Alfred, was the proprietor. LeRoy knew what he was going to say. Mr. Alfred wanted his shrimp when he needed them, not when it was convenient for LeRoy to bring them. He really hated to catch hell from Mr. Alfred, but there was no way out of it.

But Mr. Alfred didn't want to see him about being late with the day's delivery. Not meeting LeRoy's eyes, he said, "There's a fellow in the dining room been waiting to see you, boy."

"Somebody wants to see me?" LeRoy asked. The big, fat black man shrugged his shoulders.

"One of the little tables by the door to the kitchen," he said.

LeRoy was tempted to get back into the carryall and finish working the route, but he knew he couldn't do that.

"Thank you," he said, and walked out of Mr. Alfred's little office and across the kitchen into the dining room. There was nobody at the little tables to the left of the double doors to the kitchen, but when he looked to the right, he saw a sharply dressed man sitting at one of the tables, with a waitress in the act of taking away an empty glass and giving him a fresh drink.

It took a moment for the man to see him standing there, and a moment longer, until the man smiled, for LeRoy to recognize him. It was his father.

His father stood up, somewhat awkwardly, resting his hand on the table.

"Hello, LeRoy," he said. "You're so big I hardly recognized you."

LeRoy said nothing. The smile on his father's face vanished. Then he smiled again. He put out his hand.

After a moment's hesitation, LeRoy shook his father's hand.

"I'm here to help, LeRoy," his father said.

"What do you want?" LeRoy asked.

"I want to talk to you," his father said. "I told you, I'm here to help. Why don't you sit down?"

"I've got to work the route," LeRoy said. "I'm late now, as it is."

His father looked at him, and forced another smile on his face.

"I'm staying at a hotel called the Maison DuPuy in the French Quarter. You know where it is?"

"Yeah, I know where it is."

"When you finish working the route, will you come there? I'll wait for you in the bar. Will you do that, LeRoy?"

"Where'd you come from, all of a sudden?" LeRoy asked. "How'd you find me?"

"I'll tell you anything you want to know when you come to the hotel," his father said. "You will come, won't you?"

"Yeah," LeRoy said, after a moment. "I'll come. It'll be seven, seven-thirty."

"Great!" his father said. And then he looked as if he had just remembered something. "Look, if you

133

call your grandfather to tell him you're going to be late, it might not be a good idea to tell him I'm here."

LeRoy didn't answer. He turned on his heel and went back to the kitchen.

While he worked the route, LeRoy made up his mind about what to do a half-dozen different times. He chose, first of all, not to show up at the Maison DuPuy. His father had checked out of his life years ago. He had deserted LeRoy and his mother, and he had no right to come back.

Then LeRoy decided to call the old man, tell him what had happened, and ask him what to do. But he knew what the old man would say. The old man would tell him to get into the carryall and come home. The old man really had it in for his father.

And then he decided he should go to the hotel and really tell his father off. His father had run out on his mother and him, and he had no right to just walk back into his life.

But his father had said he was here to help.

At half-past seven, LeRoy drove into a parking garage just off Canal Street and turned the car over to a parking attendant. That was going to cost at least three bucks, even if he stayed only ten minutes, but it was better to spend the three bucks and make sure nobody busted in the vent window and ripped off the coolers.

When he walked through the hotel lobby toward the bar, LeRoy felt the eyes of the desk clerk on him. He felt out of place in his khaki shirt and trousers. But there was nothing to be done about that.

He pushed open the door to the bar and stood inside for a moment, until his eyes grew used to the

134

dim light. Finally, he spotted his father sitting across the room at a table. His father had seen him, too, for he stood up.

LeRoy walked across the room to his father. His father put out his hand again, and put a hand on LeRoy's shoulder.

"I can't get over how big you are," he said.

"I'm eighteen," LeRoy said. "I guess I'm about full grown."

"Sit down, sit down," his father said. It was a fancy bar. Instead of chairs, there were two-seat couches on either side of the table. A waitress appeared.

"Another scotch for me," LeRoy's father said. "What'll you have, LeRoy? A Coke? Seven-up?"

"I'll have a glass of red wine, please," LeRoy said. He didn't really want a glass of wine; what he wanted was to make sure his father understood he wasn't a little boy anymore.

His father chuckled. "Pop's turned you into a regular wine-drinking Cajun, has he?" he said.

LeRoy looked at the table. There was a fancy ashtray on it, and in the ashtray were cigarettes with lipstick on them. Half a dozen cigarette butts, and half of those had lipstick on them. When the waitress bent over and scooped up the ashtray and dumped it, LeRoy knew his father had been sitting with a woman. He had ordered "another" scotch. That meant he hadn't sat down just before LeRoy walked in.

"You said you were going to tell me what you're doing here," LeRoy said.

His father extended his package of cigarettes. LeRoy shook his head.

"Good for you," his father said. "I wish I'd never started smoking."

LeRoy didn't say anything. He waited for his father to go on.

"Well, what happened is this," his father said. "A friend of mine, in Chicago, saw the story in the newspaper and clipped it out and sent it to me." He took a wallet out of his inside jacket pocket, removed a newspaper clipping, and handed it to LeRoy.

The article was short. It said that the Chicago police had announced that they had located a material witness, LeRoy Chambers, aged eighteen, to the murder of Mrs. Sarah-Mae Carson in the Hoover Housing Project. It was the first time LeRoy had ever seen his name in newspaper type.

"You want to tell me about it?" his father asked.

"There's nothing to tell," LeRoy said. "I got off the elevator, and those guys were working her over with a knife. She saw me, and told the cops she had seen me."

"She accused you?"

"No," LeRoy said. "She just said I saw what happened."

"The smart thing would have been to keep your mouth shut," his father said. "I guess you know that."

"I know that," LeRoy said. The waitress showed up with the drinks.

"That'll be $3.25," she said. His father took a five-dollar bill from a wad and laid it on her little tray, waving away the change.

Big spender, LeRoy thought. He also noticed that his father was well dressed. There was a watch with a gold band on his wrist, and a diamond ring (at least it looked like a diamond) on his finger. He sure didn't look like he was on welfare, or digging ditches.

"So when I got the clipping," LeRoy's father said, "I figured you were probably in trouble, and that I should try to help you."

"We were in trouble when you took off on us," LeRoy said. "Where have you been, anyway?"

"I've been living in New York," his father said. "I live in New York."

"What do you do?" LeRoy asked.

"I'm a businessman," his father said.

"What kind of a businessman?" LeRoy asked.

"I buy things and I sell things," his father replied. It was obvious that he wasn't going to tell LeRoy what he was doing for a living. Whatever it was, he was making money at it.

"So how did you find me?" LeRoy asked.

"I had a friend ask around," his father said. "I called him and asked him to find out what he could."

"Why didn't you call me?" LeRoy asked.

"I tried," he said. "You didn't have a telephone."

"We couldn't afford one," LeRoy said. He realized that it sounded like an accusation, and then he thought, so what if it did. The reason they couldn't afford a telephone was that he had run off on them.

"Anyway, my friend called back and told me you and your mother had moved out of the project, and that you had apparently left town. So I figured you would probably be down here. And you are."

"How'd you know I'd be at Alfred's?" LeRoy asked.

"I delivered shrimp and crabs to Alfred's when I was your age," his father said. "I figured if he was still in business, Pop would still be selling him shrimp and crabs." He sounded proud that he had figured that out.

LeRoy just looked at his father.

"How's Pop?" his father asked.

"All right," LeRoy said. "Why didn't you come to Pass Christian? Or call up there? The old man's got a phone."

"Look," his father said, his patience worn thin, "I've had problems with your mother, and I've had problems with my father, and that's between us. It's really none of your business. All right?"

"The old man won't even talk about you," LeRoy said. "Did you know that?"

"I didn't," his father said. "But it doesn't surprise me. Pop never heard of gray. Everything's either black or white. Don't tell me he hasn't given you 'the world's full of sin and wickedness' business."

LeRoy had to smile. His father saw it, and for the first time, his father's smile looked genuine.

"Let's just say that Pop figures I'm full of sin and wickedness," his father said, "and let it go at that. Let's get back to you. What are you going to do about it?"

"What am I going to do about what?"

"About that business in Chicago. I guess you know what happens if you testify against people."

"Yeah, I know," LeRoy said. "But there's nothing I can do about it."

"There's one thing you can do," his father said. "Keep out of it. Don't testify. Tell the cops you didn't see a thing."

"I tried that," LeRoy said. "It didn't work. Anyway, I'm a material witness. They're going to make me go back up there."

"Let's just make sure we really know what we're talking about," his father said. "How do you know you're a material witness?"

"Because Sheriff Greenhaw told me I am, that's how," LeRoy said. "As a matter of fact, I'm out on bond."

"Greenhaw?" his father asked. "You don't happen to know his first name, do you? I used — "

"It's your friend," LeRoy interrupted him. "He told me you used to work on shrimp boats together."

"I'll be damned," his father said. "Ellwood Greenhaw. I haven't thought about him in years. And he's the sheriff?"

"He looks just like that sheriff in the TV advertisements," LeRoy said. "Only he's bigger. And looks meaner."

"How much is your bond?" LeRoy's father asked.

"Ten dollars," LeRoy said.

"*Ten* dollars?"

"That's it," LeRoy said.

"And that doesn't tell you anything?"

"Tell me anything about what?"

"That's like coming right out and telling you to jump bail," his father said.

"And then what would I do?" LeRoy asked.

"Come to New York with me," his father said. "We've got an extra bedroom in the apartment."

LeRoy's heart jumped. It was a way out of the whole mess. But what he replied was: "*We've* got an extra bedroom?"

His father didn't say anything for a moment. Then he shrugged his shoulders.

"I've got a lady," he said. "A very nice lady."

"You're still married to my mother," LeRoy said.

"Yeah, and I can't get a divorce, either," his father said. "The minute I try to get a divorce, she'll find out where I am, and I'll get socked with six years of child-support payments. That may not be very nice, but that's the way it is."

LeRoy suddenly became furious.

"I've got to go to the men's room," he said. He got up and left. But he didn't go to the men's room. He walked right across the hotel lobby back to the parking garage. He got into the carryall and drove back to Pass Christian.

CHAPTER
13

LeRoy decided he would not tell the old man that he had seen his father in New Orleans. He was more than a little afraid of what the old man's reaction would be.

The old man didn't ask him where he had been. After a while, LeRoy realized that seeing his father twice, first in Alfred's restaurant and then in the bar in the Maison DuPuy Hotel, hadn't taken more than half an hour. The old man had no reason to suspect that LeRoy had done anything but work the route.

When he went to bed, instead of falling asleep the way he usually did, the minute his head hit the pillow, he lay in the dark, thinking about what had happened. He was ashamed of himself for just taking off the way he had. He had sneaked away. He hadn't had the courage to tell his father what he was thinking. But hearing that his father had not only a "lady" but also an apartment with an extra bedroom, had really made him mad.

He hadn't often thought of what had happened to his father since he'd disappeared. The subject was too painful. But when he had thought about his father, he hadn't thought of him doing all right in New York, with a gold watch and a diamond ring. He had thought that his father was on welfare somewhere, and that he hadn't been in touch because he was ashamed that he couldn't give them any money.

LeRoy was sorry that he hadn't gotten his father's address. He could give it to his mother, and she could send the cops after him to collect the child-support money. If he had enough money to buy expensive jewelry and to maintain an apartment and another woman, he should have had enough money to send something to his family. At least a couple of bucks every once in a while. He remembered his father waving away all the change from the five-dollar bill. LeRoy thought of many times when a dollar and a half would have meant meat for supper, instead of a cheese-and-noodle dinner.

Was that the reason the old man was so sore about his father? Did the old man know all the time that his father was in New York, making good money? For that matter, why hadn't the old man sent them a couple of bucks when they were so broke? He knew the answer to that. His mother had never asked for it. If she had asked the old man, he would have helped them out.

Still, his father had come to help him when he heard he was in trouble. He'd come all the way down from New York to New Orleans. And, unlike the old man, his father understood the trouble he was in with the Wolves. He knew what kind of people they were.

His father seemed to know the score. Could he have been right about Sheriff Greenhaw hinting that LeRoy should take off? That was kind of hard to accept, but it was possible. If the sheriff was really on the side of the cops, why hadn't he just locked him up? Or gotten the old man to put up enough bond to make sure LeRoy would show up when the Chicago cops wanted him? He had explained what he had done, but maybe he had to say something like that. He could hardly have come out and said, "I'm setting your bond at ten bucks so you won't lose much if you take off." On the other hand, Sheriff Greenhaw believed there was no place for LeRoy to run to. As far as he knew, LeRoy had no idea where his father was. And where else could he go?

Every time LeRoy dropped off to sleep that night, he dreamed he was back in the corridor of the Hoover Project, with the Wolves standing around him, slashing at his leather jacket. He hated himself for being such a coward, but that didn't seem to change things much. He still didn't want to face the Wolves again. Those jerks had nothing better to do than hold a grudge. Getting back at him gave them something to live for.

When he finally fell into a deep sleep, he slept like a log. He didn't wake up until the old man came into his room and shook him.

"What did you eat in New Orleans?" the old man asked him, when LeRoy sat up. "One of those artificial hamburgers?"

"What are you talking about?"

"You kept me awake most of the night, talking in

143

your sleep," the old man said. "You were sure mad at somebody. I thought it must be something you ate."

"I didn't eat anything at all in New Orleans," LeRoy said. "I was late working the route and there wasn't time."

"You'll be a lot happier in your life if you learn that there's always time to sleep and eat," the old man said. "They could have waited another half an hour for the shrimp."

"I suppose," LeRoy said. For the first time, he looked up at the ceiling. The rafters were covered with plasterboard. "I see you got the roof up," he said.

"That's the ceiling," the old man said. "The roof is on the *out*side."

"What do you do about the cracks?" LeRoy asked.

"You get a guy to come in and fill them," the old man said. "They call him a 'mud man' and he walks around on stilts. I'm too old for that. There are some things you have to have an expert do."

"They get a lot of money?"

"They're in a sellers' market," the old man said. "You need them, and they know you can't do it yourself, so they charge just about what they feel like charging. The only thing you can do is stick around and watch them, so they don't smoke too many cigarettes or drink too much coffee while you're paying them fifteen dollars an hour."

"Where are you getting all the money to pay for this?" LeRoy asked, as he got out of bed.

"That's really none of your business," the old man said, "but I'll tell you, anyway. Some of it I had, and

144

some of it I had to borrow. It cost me a lot more than I thought it would. I took out a mortgage at the Savings and Loan."

"How are you going to pay it back?" LeRoy asked.

"That will be a lot harder than it was to borrow it," the old man said. "But we can make it, God willing, and if you don't drive the carryall into Lake Pontchartrain." The old man changed the subject. "What do you want for breakfast?"

"Doesn't matter," LeRoy said, pulling on his pants.

"In that case, you can have a glass of water and a piece of stale bread," the old man said, and walked out of the room.

Later, on the way into New Orleans, LeRoy wondered what his father had done in the bar at the Maison DuPuy Hotel when he hadn't come back. His feelings had probably been hurt. And he'd probably been mad. Both. LeRoy was ashamed of the way he'd sneaked off, without saying a word. But when he thought about that a while, he was able to convince himself that he wasn't the only one who had reason to be ashamed. All he had done was walk away from his father in a bar. His father had walked away from his family, leaving them to feed themselves and put a roof over their heads any way they could, while he went to New York and got himself another woman and a big apartment and a lot of flashy jewelry.

LeRoy decided that after his father knew he wasn't coming back to the bar, he'd had two choices. He could have come to Pass Christian and faced him and the old man, or he could have gone upstairs to his "lady" and told her they were going back to New York.

The last thing LeRoy expected his father to do was what he did: He was waiting for him again at Alfred's restaurant. He was even sitting at the same table. But now he had his lady with him.

LeRoy had pictured her in his mind as a floozie, all dressed up, with a lot of makeup. She wasn't that way at all. She looked like a very nice person.

But LeRoy didn't have much time to look at her. The minute he stepped into the dining room, his father saw him. He got up immediately and walked over to LeRoy.

"I want to talk to you," his father said, putting his hand on his arm, holding him. "And this time, by God, you're going to hear what I have to say."

He sort of pushed LeRoy back through the door into the kitchen, then through the kitchen and out to the alley. LeRoy remembered that his father used to deliver shrimp and crabs here. He knew his way around the kitchen as well as LeRoy did.

Around the corner from Alfred's was another restaurant, a little one, a run-down place with a counter and half a dozen tables. Without taking his hand off LeRoy's arm, his father led him into it and then to a table. He called out to a waitress to bring coffee.

"I guess you thought I'd be halfway back to New York by now, huh?" his father said. LeRoy didn't answer him.

"I almost left," his father went on, "after you took off yesterday. But then I realized that what you had done was dumb, and the reason you did it was because I hadn't taught you any better."

LeRoy, for just a moment, met his father's eyes. Then he looked away again.

"And I figured that since I'd come all the way down here, it would be stupid of me to go back without telling you what I came to tell you," his father said. "So you just sit there, LeRoy, and listen to me."

LeRoy looked up at his father and met his eyes again.

"You pay attention to me, now," his father said. "I told you that a friend of mine sent me that clipping, and that I called him up and asked him to look around for you."

"You told me that," LeRoy said.

"I didn't tell you everything he told me," his father said.

"Like what?"

"Like those guys, the Wolves, have really got it in for you," his father said. "And I don't mean they just have their feelings hurt, either, because you squealed on them. They're out to get you, son. You understand what I'm telling you?"

"I know that," LeRoy said.

"I don't think you really hear what I'm saying to you," his father said. "Let me tell you about my friend. He's not a very nice man. He's been in prison, the whole business. He's a very tough character. You understand what I'm saying?"

"No, I guess I don't," LeRoy said.

"He knows people, people who know the Wolves. He can find out things even the cops can't find out. And what he found out is that the Wolves have made a decision about you. As far as they're concerned, it's very simple. If you go to court, if you just go to the grand jury, they're going to go to jail. If they get the wrong judge, they're going to get life. The best they can expect is that they're going to get sent up for twenty years, which probably means seven or eight years in jail. You understand that?"

"They killed that old lady," LeRoy said. "They didn't have to use a knife on her."

"But they did. And they're going to go to jail for it. If you testify. If you're dead, you can't testify. As far as they're concerned, it's as simple as that."

"They're in jail."

"The three of them who did in the old lady are in jail," his father said. "The rest of them are outside."

"The cops are going to protect me," LeRoy said.

"What makes you think that the cops care one way or the other what happens to you?" his father asked.

"I'm their only witness," LeRoy said.

"Let's say you testify, right? And they send those guys up. The minute that happens, the cops couldn't care less about you. And all of the rest of the Wolves will be out to get you for putting their friends away."

"I thought about all of that," LeRoy said. "I don't think they'll come all the way down here after me."

"But you don't know, do you?"

"What are you telling me?"

"I'm telling you not to testify, to get out of here, and to come to New York," his father said.

"And what am I supposed to do in New York?" LeRoy asked.

"What are you going to do down here, spend the rest of your life up to your elbows in stinking shrimp?"

"It's a living," LeRoy said. "It sure beats making salads in the Del Monte Cafeteria."

"There are two kinds of people in this world, LeRoy," his father said. "There are the kind who work with their backs, and the kind who work with their heads. I work with my head. I live pretty well."

"What exactly do you do?"

His father, who had been sitting on the edge of his chair, leaning his elbow on the table, now sat back.

"You know what the numbers are?" he asked.

"You're running numbers?" LeRoy asked. LeRoy knew what the numbers were. A guy came around, and you gave him half a dollar, and he gave you a number. If your number came up, you won five hundred dollars. The trouble was that you had about one chance in ten thousand to have your number come up. It was a racket, and it took advantage of poor people.

"I started out as a runner," his father said. "Now I've got four guys who run numbers for me."

LeRoy stared at his father.

"Don't look down your nose at me, boy," his father said. "Don't start getting righteous like Pop, with his sin and wickedness. Unless he's changed a whole lot, he's not above putting a couple of bucks on the horses when he feels like it."

LeRoy remembered the horse named Instant Expert and how the old man had won a lot of money betting on him.

"The people who play numbers want to play numbers," his father said. "Nobody goes in there with a gun and takes their fifty cents away from them. It's the only chance they have to make a little money."

"So you want me to come to New York and run numbers for you?" LeRoy asked.

"I want you to come to New York to keep from getting your throat cut," his father said. "If you're too good to run numbers, suit yourself. But the guys who run numbers for me make two, three hundred a week. Which I know is a lot more than you'll ever make hauling stinking shrimp coolers around back alleys."

"And if I don't want to run numbers, then what?" LeRoy asked.

"Then you get yourself any kind of a job you want," his father said. "Hell, you want to go to college? So go to college. I'll pay for it."

LeRoy was quiet for a moment. Then he said, "I think you're wrong about one thing. I don't think Sheriff Greenhaw was telling me to run away. I think if I took off, he'd come looking for me."

"Use your head," his father said impatiently. "The only reason the cops are interested in you is because you're a witness. If you don't show up to testify before that grand jury, they won't have a case, and if they don't have a case, they won't need you. In six months, they will have forgotten all about you."

"And for six months, they'll be looking for me," LeRoy said.

"They've been looking for me for five years and they haven't found me," his father said.

"What are they looking for you for?" LeRoy asked, suddenly very curious.

"Your mother turned them loose on me," his father said. "Yeah, your sainted mother. She signed a warrant against me."

"For what?"

"For child support, what else?" his father said. "How she figured I'd be able to pay child support if I was in jail, I don't know. But she signed the warrant."

"How come, if you're making so much money, you never did send any?" LeRoy asked.

"I figured if she got a money order from New York, she'd tell the cops," his father said.

"All you would have had to do was put money in an envelope," LeRoy said. "Or have your friend in Chicago mail it in Chicago."

"What's done is done, all right?" his father said, and LeRoy saw that he was angry. LeRoy knew he had asked a question his father couldn't answer. His father was wrong. Not sending them money when he had money was rotten.

But that didn't change what his father had to say about the Wolves. He was right about that. The Wolves were not only mad at him, they were crazy. It wouldn't bother them one bit to stick a knife in him. And it was pretty clear that if they did catch him, they wouldn't just beat him up.

There was a long silence between them. LeRoy thought his father was trying either to keep from getting mad or to come up with a better explanation for not sending his family money. But maybe he was only trying to decide what to do next.

"To tell you the truth," his father said finally, "I guess I thought the minute I showed up here, you'd be so glad to get out of your trouble that you'd hop on the first plane with me. And for a while I couldn't understand what was the matter with you. But I think I know. You've been living with Pop, and lis-

151

tening to Pop, and I know what Pop's been telling you. 'Do right. Put the bad guys in jail. Do your duty.' I'm not saying he's wrong, either. In Pass Christian, Mississippi, he's right. But he just doesn't understand Chicago. Or anything else outside Pass Christian."

LeRoy looked at his father without saying anything.

"So, I'll tell you what I'm going to do," his father said. He reached into his pocket and pulled out a wad of bills held together with a gold money clip in the shape of a dollar sign. He slid the clip off, slipped out four fifty-dollar bills, and laid them on the table.

Just like the old man, LeRoy thought. A bundle of money, in fifty-dollar bills. The difference was that the old man worked hard for his.

His father took a gold felt-tip pen from his pocket and wrote something on a napkin.

"That's my address and my telephone number," his father said. "If you want to turn it over to your mother, I don't suppose there's anything I can do about that."

LeRoy looked at him in surprise.

"What I hope you'll do," his father said, "is think about the trouble you're in. And decide to come to New York. At least until this thing blows over. If you don't like it up there, you can come back."

"I don't know what to say."

"I'm your father," his father said. "I'm trying to help you. I hope you understand that. I mean, I hope you don't give that address to your mother."

"What could I tell her?" LeRoy asked. "About where I was, I mean."

"You couldn't tell her, or Pop, where you were," his father said. "You know that. You tell either one of them, they'll tell the cops, and we'll both be behind bars."

LeRoy hadn't touched the money or the napkin with the address on it. He looked down at the table.

"Go on, put it in your wallet," his father said. "And think it over before you do anything. I mean, if you do come to New York, you won't be able to change your mind and come back. Right away, I mean. If you come to New York, you'll have to stay there until this thing blows over. Six months, maybe a year."

"I wouldn't be able to tell Momma where I was for a year?"

"You could write her," his father said. "But you couldn't tell her where you were. I want you to understand that."

"And what if the cops decide that the only place I'm likely to be is with you?" LeRoy asked.

"They don't know that you know where I am, so they won't think of that. And, like I said, they've been looking for me for years and haven't found me. You don't have to worry."

LeRoy didn't say anything for a long time. Then he said, "I got to work the route." He stood up, putting the napkin and money in his pocket as he did.

His father stood up awkwardly, and then put his hand out to LeRoy.

"I may not be the father you want," he said. "But I'm doing the best I know how."

LeRoy put out his hand and took his father's.

"Thank you," he said. He felt like crying. He let go of his father's hand and started out of the little restaurant.

"Take care of yourself, son," his father called after him.

CHAPTER
14

The last stop on the route was Le Cruet, where the executive chef was Joe Keller, the man who had provided champagne for the celebration of the new roof.

LeRoy turned the shrimp over to the fish chef and waited until he had examined the shrimp closely, making sure they were as fresh as LeRoy had said. When he was satisfied that they were, the fish chef told LeRoy that Mr. Keller wanted to see him. He jerked his thumb toward the dining room.

It was the first time LeRoy had ever seen Joe Keller dressed in anything but chef's whites. He was now wearing a dark blue business suit and a really bright white shirt. But that wasn't the most surprising thing. The old man, wearing the same suit he'd worn the morning he'd picked LeRoy up at the bus terminal, was sitting at the table with him. There was a wine bottle on the table between them.

"Finally," the old man greeted him. "And a good thing. If I had any more of this wine, I'd have to crawl back to Pass Christian."

"Hello, Mr. Keller," LeRoy said, and then, to the old man, "What are you doing here?"

"Ve're going to Canal Street to gedt you a zoot," Joe Keller said.

"You'll need it for Chicago," the old man said. "And when I thought about it, I realized that if I let you pick one out yourself, you'd come back looking like either a gambler or a fugitive from a circus."

"You're troo growing, I vould kess?" Joe Keller asked.

"I haven't grown any lately," LeRoy said.

"Goot, den ve ken gedt you a goot zoot. A goot zoot you can haf for years." He stood up. "You vant to come vid us, Aaron, or you vant to sidt here and haf annuder boddle vine?"

"I'm going," the old man said, drinking the last of the wine in his glass. He got up.

From the way he greeted Mr. Keller, it was easy to tell that the salesman knew him pretty well. And it was just as easy to tell that he didn't know what Mr. Keller was doing with two black men, one in work clothes and the other one in a suit that must have been new about the time of World War II.

"Vat ve need is a nize zoot of clodes for my friend," Mr. Keller said, "zo dot he vill make a nize imprezzion in court." Then he decided he had better explain that. "He didn't do nudding. Vat he is, is a vitness."

"I think I have just the thing, Mr. Keller," the salesman said. He measured LeRoy around the shoulders and the waist. And then he went to a rack

156

for an almost black suit with a faint pinstripe, which he displayed over his arm.

"Dot vould make him look like an undertaker," Joe Keller said. "Gedt him a nize gray zoot."

The salesman came back with a gray suit, also with a pinstripe. Joe Keller nodded his approval. The salesman held the jacket for LeRoy to put on. It fitted just about perfectly. LeRoy was delighted until he glanced at the sleeve and saw the price tag: $230. The old man didn't have that kind of money.

"I like dot," Joe Keller announced. "You like dot, Aaron?"

"He still looks like an undertaker," the old man said. "But I like it better than the black one."

"Zee if duh pants fit," Joe Keller ordered.

"It costs $230," LeRoy protested.

"Plus the tax," the salesman said. He obviously thought $230 was a cheap price for a suit like that.

"I gedt it for you wholezale," Joe Keller said. "I godt a deal vid the boss."

"I believe the discount applies only to family members, Mr. Keller," the salesman said.

"You go gedt duh boss," Joe Keller ordered. "And, LeRoy, you go zee if duh pants fit."

When LeRoy came out of the changing room, holding up the pants (which were loose in the waist) with one hand, he saw another man standing there, obviously the boss. The man motioned for LeRoy to get up on a little upholstered stool, and marked how much of the trousers were to be taken in. Then he pinned up the cuffs.

"That should do it," he said. "That's a nice suit."

LeRoy was delighted. He was going to get the suit wholesale. It was a fine set of threads.

"If you've got one that'll fit me," the old man suddenly said, "same terms, I'll have a look at it."

The man who was the boss looked a little pained. Joe Keller laughed.

"Don't look dot vay," he said. "Duh next time you come by duh restaurant, I'll gif you a boddle goot vine. And, anyvay, all doze shrimp you eadt, vere do you tink dey come from?"

LeRoy was a little relieved when they couldn't find a gray suit exactly like his for the old man. The old man wound up with a blue pinstripe like the one Joe Keller said made LeRoy look like an undertaker.

They bought two shirts apiece and two neckties, and then, almost as an afterthought, dress shoes to go with the suits. They took the shirts and ties and shoes with them. The suits would be ready the next day.

As they walked back to Le Cruet, the old man took his wad of money from his pocket.

"What do they give you off, Joe?" the old man asked. "Twenty percent?"

"Tirty-fife," Joe Keller said. "Pudt your money avay. Ve'll vork somezing oudt vid duh shrimp."

"I appreciate this, Joe," the old man said. "Tell Mr. Keller thank you, boy."

"Thanks, Mr. Keller," LeRoy said.

"Forget it," Joe Keller said. "Ledt me tell you somezing aboudt your grandfadder, LeRoy. Ven I vas stardting oudt, dere vas a lodt of times ven I didn't haf duh money to pay for duh shrimp. Your grandfadder gafe me credit ven nobody else vould. Ven I gedt a chanze to do him a liddle fafor — my pleasure."

They rode back to Pass Christian at forty miles an

hour, with LeRoy driving the truck behind the old man in the carryall. Either the old man wasn't kidding about having had too much wine, or he was just not taking any chances.

Driving that slowly gave LeRoy a chance to do a little thinking.

As nice as the suit was, it wasn't any nicer than the clothes his father had been wearing. And his father probably had many more suits than the ones LeRoy had seen him in. The old man had one suit — which had probably been around as long as LeRoy. And the old man worked, worked hard all the time.

His father had said that his numbers runners made two, three hundred a week. If LeRoy went to New York, his father had told him he could have a job running numbers. He would be able to have a closet full of clothes like this.

He felt ashamed of himself. The old man had just bought him the best (and for that matter, the first) suit he'd ever had in his life, and here he was thinking the old man was a fool for working so hard for so little.

And then he wondered why the old man had bought himself a suit. Did the old man plan to go to Chicago with him? Is that why he bought the clothes? That would be all I need, LeRoy thought, having the old man in Chicago with me. In addition to keeping the Wolves from cutting my throat, I'd have to watch out for the old man.

When they got to the house, LeRoy asked him. "How come you bought a suit?"

"Why shouldn't I buy a suit?" the old man snapped. "I work hard for my money, and if I want to buy a suit, or for that matter, a Cadillac automobile, that's my business."

"Are you coming to Chicago with me?" LeRoy asked.

"Sure," the old man said sarcastically. "And who would work the route? The tooth fairy?"

"Well, you don't have to jump down my throat," LeRoy said. "I was just asking."

"Okay," the old man said. "No, I am not going to Chicago with you. And the reason I bought the suit is that it looked like a bargain to me. I always try to take advantage of a bargain when I see one. And I suppose another reason is, while I was sitting there waiting for you, Joe Keller kept pouring wine down me. I was feeling pretty good."

"I saw that," LeRoy said. "Him sitting on your shoulders, forcing you to drink all that wine."

"That's the trouble with those Austrians," the old man said. "Do them a little favor, and they spend the rest of your life trying to get you drunk."

"You can take one look at Joe Keller and tell he's full of sin and wickedness," LeRoy said.

"That's Mr. Keller to you, boy. Don't ever let me hear you call him Joe," the old man said. "And don't you be joking about sin and wickedness. There's enough of it around."

The next night, when LeRoy got home from New Orleans with their suits in boxes, he found that the old man had bought a long mirror and hung it on the inside of his bedroom door.

"I figured you'd want to look in the mirror and fall in love with yourself," he said.

"I may do just that," LeRoy said, and started to unwrap his suit. The old man watched him just long enough to see that he was serious, and then he left the room. LeRoy put on one of his shirts and a necktie, and even the new shoes. And he looked at himself in the mirror.

"Don't hog the mirror," the old man said. LeRoy looked at the reflection of the old man, wearing his new suit.

The old man examined himself carefully.

"You know what we look like?" he asked.

"You tell me," LeRoy said.

"Butch Cassidy and the Sundance Kid," the old man said. LeRoy looked at him, not knowing what he meant. "I mean the real ones, not the movie stars," the old man said. "I saw a picture of them, the real ones. They'd robbed a bank or something, and gone to Saint Louis and bought a bunch of fancy clothes and had their picture took. They looked like a bunch of cowboys all dressed up. What you and me look like is a couple of shrimpers all dressed up."

"I think I look more like a politician," LeRoy said.

The old man snorted.

"Now that we're all dressed up," he said, "it seems kind of a shame to waste it. Let's go out and buy our dinner."

"Yeah," LeRoy said. "Let's do that."

They drove along the beachfront highway until they came to Angelo's Steak and Rib House.

"Pull in there," the old man said. "They charge a fortune, but the food's good, and if we've gone this far, we might as well go whole hog."

When they finally sat down to eat, LeRoy thought that while the restaurant might be expensive, they

161

weren't making much money off the old man. There was a help-yourself soup-and-salad bar, and the way the old man helped himself, he wiped out whatever profit the restaurant had hoped to make.

They had just about finished their large slice of standing rib of beef when Sheriff Greenhaw appeared. "Can I sit down?" he asked.

"Help yourself, Ellwood," the old man said. "You want a cup of coffee or something? LeRoy and I are throwing our money away like a couple of drunken sailors."

"You look like a couple of bankers," Sheriff Greenhaw said. He caught a waitress's eye and signaled for a cup of coffee. "I was on my way out to your place when I saw the carryall," he said.

"I figured that's what had happened," the old man said. "They want LeRoy, right?"

LeRoy's stomach started to hurt.

"Yeah, they called up about four o'clock. I was over in Alabama, getting a guy from the Mobile jail. I got the message when I came back about an hour ago."

"When?" LeRoy asked.

"They were going to send somebody down after him tomorrow," Sheriff Greenhaw said. "I told them not to bother. If I can't get one of my men a plane ride at the taxpayers' expense, I'm not about to let one of theirs have one, either." He looked at LeRoy. "So I called up there and told them I would put you on a plane tomorrow, LeRoy."

"Oh, hell," LeRoy said.

"You knew it was coming, boy," the old man said. "What time are you going to come for him, Ellwood?"

"There's a plane at half-past two," Sheriff Greenhaw said. "I figured you could put him on that."

He reached into his trousers pocket and laid an airplane ticket on the table.

"I could take him in when I start to work the route," the old man said. "There will be time."

"A policeman will meet you at the airport in Chicago, LeRoy," the sheriff said. "And they'll put you up in a hotel overnight. The next day you go before the grand jury. And as soon as that's over, they'll put you on a plane back here."

"If I don't have my throat cut by then," LeRoy said.

"Now, that's not going to happen," Sheriff Greenhaw said. "They're going to take care of you, LeRoy. You have my word on that."

The old man picked up the ticket and put it in his jacket pocket.

"He'll be on the plane, Ellwood," he said.

"You call me from the airport, Mr. Aaron," Sheriff Greenhaw said. "And then I'll call up there to make sure somebody meets him."

"And what if nobody meets me?" LeRoy asked.

"Somebody will meet you," Sheriff Greenhaw said. "There's nothing to worry about on that account."

"And if nobody does, then what?"

The old man gave him a dirty look. He wasn't supposed to challenge Sheriff Greenhaw.

"It's all right, Mr. Aaron," Sheriff Greenhaw said. "If for some reason nobody meets you, you just walk up to the first cop you see and tell him that you're a material witness in a homicide, and that you were supposed to be met, and nobody showed up. Okay?"

"Yes, sir," LeRoy said, without much conviction.

Strawberry shortcake was included with the dinner. LeRoy had saved room for it. Now he didn't even want to think about eating it.

From then on, the night seemed like a bad dream. They went back to the house, and the old man announced that he was tired. The only reference he made to what was going on was to tell LeRoy he might as well wear the same shirt on the airplane, and save the other new one to wear before the grand jury.

Then he went to bed, and in just a couple of minutes, LeRoy could hear him snoring. The old man really snored.

LeRoy packed a bag with extra underwear and socks and some ordinary clothes. Then he took a shower and tried to sleep.

He wished his father had never shown up down here. If he hadn't, and if there weren't a way out of going back to Chicago, he would just get on the plane without another thought.

But now he didn't have to go to Chicago and risk getting his throat cut. He had somewhere else to go, where neither the Wolves nor the cops would find him. And he had the money to take him there. At one time, there would have been no doubt in his mind that New York would be the place to go.

So why was he going to Chicago? Why had he known all along, even as he'd put his father's money in his pocket, that he wasn't going to New York? Because of the old man, that's why, old "sin and wickedness" himself. To the old man, everything was black and white. If LeRoy were to do something he thought was wrong, then he would consider LeRoy bad. The old man would cut him off just as surely and finally as he had cut off his own son. If LeRoy took off for any place but Chicago, he could forget about ever coming back to Pass Christian.

Well, then, so what if he were shut out by some old Pass Christian, Mississippi, shrimp fisherman? Wasn't that better than getting his throat cut?

The answer to that was clear. LeRoy couldn't live with the idea of having the old man shut him out of his life. He needed the old man. And the old man needed him, too, even if he wouldn't admit it. The old man must have been pretty lonely before LeRoy came down from Chicago, and he would be even lonelier if LeRoy left. He couldn't work the route by himself. And if he couldn't work the route, he wouldn't be able to pay back the money he'd borrowed to rebuild the house. What would happen then? He would lose the house, that's what would happen.

I'm not brave, LeRoy decided, about going back up there and testifying against those guys. It's that I'm more afraid of the old man cutting me off, shutting me out of his life, than I am of all the Wolves in the project, and all their friends and relatives, too.

His father would not understand that. His father would think he was a fool. And maybe he was. But he and the old man needed each other. So if he had to play by the old man's black-and-white rules, he'd play by the old man's black-and-white rules.

There just better be a cop waiting for me, he thought, when I get off that airplane in Chicago, that's all.

The next morning was like every other morning. He woke up to the sound of the old man brushing his teeth and gargling. When he gargled, he sounded like a storm sewer. They had breakfast. Then LeRoy went down to the wharf and iced down the shrimp.

The only difference was that he quit early, about half-past eleven, when the old man waved at him from the house. Also, he changed into his new suit, instead of into the khaki uniform he usually wore to New Orleans. And the old man was with him in the carryall.

He didn't know how to get to the airport, and the old man had to give him directions. When they got there, the old man asked, "You want me to come in with you?"

LeRoy replied without thinking, "I've never been in an airport before."

"Okay," the old man said. "Then put this thing in the parking lot." After a moment he added, "There's not a whole hell of a lot of difference between an airport and a bus station, when you think about it."

The old man insisted on carrying LeRoy's suitcase into the airport, and he led him to the ticket window. The old man handed the ticket clerk the ticket.

"You're LeRoy Chambers?" the ticket clerk asked.

"I'm his grandfather," the old man said.

"Flight 127 will be boarding from Gate 6 in fifteen minutes," the clerk said, and gave the ticket back to the old man. The old man handed it to LeRoy.

"Don't lose it," the old man said.

"I'll see what I can do," LeRoy said, angry that he was being treated like a little boy.

They walked through the terminal to Gate 6. They sat in silence for a couple of minutes. Then the old man reached into his pocket and came out with his wad of money.

"Almost forgot," he said, giving LeRoy two fifty-dollar bills. "Try not to lose it," he said.

"Thank you," LeRoy said.

The loudspeaker went off. Eastern Airlines announced that Flight 127, Whisper-Jet service to Saint Louis and Chicago, was ready for boarding.

"Well, that's it," the old man said. He stood up. "You better go get on it." He put out his hand and shook LeRoy's. And then he said, "I expect you can find a plane in Saint Louis to take you to New York."

LeRoy looked at him for a long moment before he knew what the old man was talking about.

"Alfred called me ten minutes after your daddy walked in his door," the old man said.

LeRoy's eyes filled with tears, and he had trouble talking.

"Grandpa," he said finally, with effort, "I never was going to go with him."

There were tears in the old man's eyes, too.

"Well, I'm glad to hear that, LeRoy," he said. "I'm truly glad to hear that. When you never said anything about seeing your daddy, I figured — you know what I figured."

"Well, you figured wrong, old man," LeRoy said angrily. "You're not right all the time."

And then they were hugging each other. And the old man said hoarsely, "I'm damn glad I was wrong this time."

Then, as if the emotion embarrassed him, he pushed LeRoy away.

"You better get on your plane," he said.

"Yeah," LeRoy said, and forced himself to smile.

"One more thing, boy," the old man said. "See if you can't talk some sense into your mother. There's no sense her living in some room in Chicago when we've got the house near built. You talk her into coming back with you."

LeRoy didn't even try to speak. He smiled and nodded and went out the gate to the airplane.

About the Author

W. E. Butterworth is the author of many books for young adults, including *Under the Influence, Slaughter by Auto,* and *Flunking Out.* Since 1960, Mr. Butterworth has devoted his time entirely to writing. Before then, he was a civilian information officer for the Army. The author lives in Fairhope, Alabama, with his wife, a former ballerina, and the youngest of their three children.